"IT WAS THE RISKIEST MISSION IN THE HISTORY OF THE ISRAELI AIR FORCE."

— A pilot who flew it

The Israeli F-16s were outfitted with two MK 84 bombs, chaff and flares, and Sidewinder missiles. For the fuel-guzzling afterburner takeoff, low altitude flight to Baghdad, 9,000 pounds of fuel would be used. There would be 1,000 pounds of fuel or 15 minutes of flying time left in the planes' tanks when they landed back in Israel—if all went well.

It would be cutting it close, especially if they had to duel in any dogfights with Iraqi MIGs.

BULLSEYE IRAQ

BULLSEYE IRAQ

Previously published as *Bullseye One Reactor*
and *Bullseye One*

DAN McKINNON

ILLUSTRATIONS
BY
EDDIE MOORE

BERKLEY BOOKS, NEW YORK

BULLSEYE IRAQ

A Berkley Book / published by arrangement with
House of Hits Publishing

PRINTING HISTORY
House of Hits edition / January 1987
Berkley edition / December 1988

ISBN: 0-425-11259-4

A BERKLEY BOOK ® TM 757,375
Berkley Books are published by The Berkley Publishing Group,
200 Madison Avenue, New York, NY 10016.
The name "BERKLEY" and the "B" logo
are trademarks belonging to Berkley Publishing Corporation.

PRINTED IN THE UNITED STATES OF AMERICA

10 9 8 7 6 5 4 3 2

ACKNOWLEDGMENTS

Since the day it happened, this is one story that has fascinated and intrigued me as well as millions of others around the world.

Tight Israeli security makes it difficult to glean details of anything their Air Force does. But now, five years after, I've been able to assemble most of the facts, thoughts, ideas and actions behind this daring and dramatic raid.

Experts around the world have helped me piece together this dramatic story.

It is only possible to tell this story because of the men of courage and dedication in the Israeli Air Force.

In a technical sense, Dick Pawloski, who works for General Dynamics and is one of the world's experts in air warfare, Electronic Counter Measures (ECM) and on the Middle East, was an invaluable help.

Capt. Ed Kosiba, a worldwide respected F-16 instructor, who is now part of the 466th Tactical Fighter Squadron at Hill Air Force Base in Salt Lake City, provided in-depth understanding of F-16 operations.

Lt. Col. Andy Crawford, ANG, an F-4 back seater, bombing and ECM specialist, aided with understanding in specialized bombing techniques.

Longtime close personal friend Cmdr. Randy Cunningham, the Navy's most decorated fighter pilot in the Vietnam War and its only MIG ace, provided keen insight in air-to-air techniques.

Gen. Ron Fogleman, Commander of the 836th Air Division (TAC), provided encouragement in ground attack tactics.

Dave Kirstein, a respected Washington lawyer, provided keen editing, just like he used to do for me when he was general counsel of the Civil Aeronautics Board (CAB) in the early 1980s.

Dr. Tim LaHaye, a best-selling Christian author and family counseling specialist, provided many helpful suggestions and ideas.

Hal Lindsey, author of *The Late Great Planet Earth* and other best-selling books about Israel, provided thoughtful ideas and counsel.

I'm grateful to Rev. Lon Solomon of McLean Bible Church in McLean, Virginia, for his expert verification of Israeli history.

My congressman, Rep. Duncan Hunter, an advocate of a strong national defense for the United States and all the free world, and his top aide, John Palafoutas, were a real help and inspiration.

Morris Nachtomi and Sam Fondiler at Tower Airlines provided efficient logistical help.

Hon. Dennis Kenneally, Deputy Assistant Secretary of The Air Force for Reserve Affairs, made helpful arrangements for me to better understand the operation of the F-16.

Margie Avila did a super job of typing and retyping the manuscript, again, again and again. Chuck Wraight, Lori Donohue and Jean Bradford did their usual outstanding job of editing and proofreading.

My dad, Clinton D. McKinnon, former U.S. congressman and newspaper publisher, did his usual constructive and painfully thorough job of bettering my spelling and grammar.

And I'd like to express my appreciation to my wife, Janice, for her patience, gentle encouragement and understanding of how much time it took to research and write this story.

Most of all, I'd like to thank a few close friends in Israel who are among the finest men I've known anywhere.

*Dedicated to
General Avihu Ben-Nun,
Commander of the Israeli Air Force,
and some very special men
of the Israeli Air Force ·
whose actions are featured in detail
in this book, but unfortunately, whose true
identities cannot be revealed.*

FOREWORD

It is a distinct honor and pleasure for me to write the foreword to this book for my friend Dan McKinnon, a naval aviation hero in his own right and the man who most epitomizes the patriotic American.

This book is about the most daring and intricate bombing raid of modern tactical warfare against the only nuclear target in history. For the reader, *Bullseye Iraq* gives you the insight of the ongoing international intrigue and deadly earnest decisions that the state of Israel combats on a daily basis.

The story is so fantastic that it would appear to be fiction. It is not. *Bullseye Iraq* is historically accurate. Having flown with the IAF, I know that the courage and dedication of the unnamed pilots depicted in this book are true representations of the heart of Israel.

Dan has captured the pure essence of history and depicts the events that brought Israel to its present day enigma. The reader could study ten books concerning the history of the Middle East and sitll not gain the insight offered in the first chapters of this book.

Stand by, the action is fast and furious as seen from the cockpit of one of the best U.S. jet fighters, the F-16. Fasten your seat belts and hold on as you ride with a strike force toward a nuclear target. Not since I flew in combat has my heart pounded with such vigor.

With the world situation as it is, would you as a U.S. citizen want Iran, Iraq or Libya to have a nuclear bomb capability? What if they were our neighbors sworn to our destruction? *Bullseye Iraq* is an historical and dramatic account of Israel's reaction to the above questions.

Commander Randy "Duke" Cunningham
Commanding Officer
U.S. Navy Aggressor Squadron
First Ace in Vietnam

Contents

1

Shocking the World

A SMALL GROUP of men huddled in a book-lined office at 3:00 P.M. Monday, June 8, 1981, listening intently to a radio playing music.

It was Shavuot—a public holiday celebrating the Feast of Pentecost, or the giving of the law to the Jewish people by God.

Outside the air-conditioned office there was a festive holiday mood as Israelis enjoyed the hot summer day.

The beaches were crowded, families were on picnics and tourists were sightseeing throughout the countryside.

It was a day of relaxation. The country was at rest and radios were providing background entertainment.

The brief hourly news summary broadcast over the radio said nothing of real interest and drifted in and out of people's consciousness.

Following the hourly newscast, music continued on the Israeli Broadcasting Service.

In his office at that instant, a short, balding, frail old man, with horn-rimmed glasses so thick it appeared he would be blind without them, went into a furious rage.

Through the thick magnifying glasses, his angry eyes appeared to be bulging out of their sockets. Standing behind his cluttered desk in his baggy pants and crisply starched open-collar dress shirt, the prime minister of

Israel demanded of his press secretary, Uri Porath, why the state radio station had failed to broadcast a statement he had personally approved and ordered broadcast at exactly 3:00 P.M.

Porath was just as dumbfounded.

An hour earlier, Porath had called KOL YISRAEL—The Voice of Israel—and personally dictated a statement to the announcer in charge of the skeleton holiday staff with instructions to broadcast it immediately.

But nothing happened.

Porath, new on the job as press aide and really unknown to the radio staffers, was now frantically searching his notes for the phone number to call the director of the state radio.

Israeli Prime Minister Menachem Begin fumed as he paced behind his desk, grumbling in frustration, "We can plan the most intricate bombing raid in history but I can't even get a simple statement on the radio."

Begin was intolerant of sloppy organization and execution of his orders. As he ranted, aides quietly shuddered to think how his fury could bring on another heart attack—possibly a fatal one this time.

The prime minister had ordered Porath to write the public statement the day before, but in a compromise agreement with Cabinet ministers, intelligence and military leaders, Begin agreed not to broadcast it until an Arab country had first broadcast news of events in Iraq.

By midday, Israeli intelligence picked up Jordanian radio reports of parliamentary debate claiming Israeli planes were cooperating in the Iran-Iraq war on the side of Iran.

This report led to Begin's decision to issue his statement. It was questionable whether the intercepted debate really referred to the news the prime minister was awaiting. But Begin decided to release the startling, dramatic news anyway.

Just as Uri Porath found the station's number, the phone in Begin's office rang.

"Hello, Uncle," said the sheepish voice of Emmanuel

Halprin, Begin's nephew and a staffer at the state radio station. "We just got this ridiculous statement from someone who claims to be your press officer. We did not broadcast it because we thought it was a joke. This is so startling, we couldn't believe it. Are you sure it is real?"

"Yes, damn it," Begin said with indignation. "Get it broadcast—*now.*"

"Yes, sir," Halprin replied.

While they waited, one of Begin's close Cabinet ministers asked, "Mr. Prime Minister, what do you think the world's reaction to your statement is going to be?"

"It doesn't matter," said Begin. "We did what was right and what we had to do for the best interests of Israel and the world."

At the radio station headquarters in Tel Aviv there was a flurry of activity.

The duty announcer was handed the statement.

He again stared at it in disbelief, but rehearsed reading it aloud to himself in the few minutes he had before reading it to the nationwide audience—and the world.

At exactly 3:30 P.M. Monday, June 8, 1981, Israeli State Radio programming was interrupted. The announcer—in a concerned and not-altogether-steady voice—read a statement that would shock the world:

"The Israel Air Force yesterday attacked and destroyed completely the Osiris nuclear reactor which is near Baghdad. . . ."

2

Never Again

DURING A CROWDED, noisy and spellbinding press conference on the Tuesday after the Sunday attack, Prime Minister Begin explained that once the Iraqi reactor became "hot" any successful bombing raid would unleash "a horrifying wave of radioactivity."

He reminded the news personnel of the grisly Holocaust deaths and how the Nazis had used poisonous Zyklon B gas on their Jewish victims.

"Radioactivity is also a poison," Begin declared. "In Baghdad, hundreds of thousands of innocent citizens would have been hurt. I for one would never have made a proposal under such circumstances to send our Air Force to bomb the reactor."

Begin outlined his "terrible dilemma."

"Should we now be passive—and then lose the last opportunity without those horrible casualties—to destroy this hotbed of death, or should we act now?"

He quickly and with great emotion answered his own question.

"Then this country and this people would have been lost, after the Holocaust."

He echoed his inner fears that "another Holocaust would have happened in the history of the Jewish people," reminding his audience of the 6 million Jews murdered by the Nazis in World War II.

"Never again! Never again!" Begin declared.

"Tell your friends, tell anybody you meet, we shall defend our people with all the means at our disposal," Begin said in his impassioned plea.

With his sense of history and his conviction of his responsibility to continue that history, Begin pressed on.

The destruction of the Iraqi nuclear bomb factory was a "morally supreme act of national self-defense. No fault whatsoever on our side," he proclaimed.

Begin charged that Iraqis planned to build three to five Hiroshima-sized atomic bombs which they intended to drop on Israel. He said such an attack would cause up to 600,000 Israeli casualties and the destruction of the nation's industrial and agricultural infrastructure.

Begin compared the deaths of 600,000 of Israel's nearly 4 million citizens to wiping out 44 million Americans or 8 million Egyptians.

The prime minister cited an article in the Iraqi newspaper *Al Thawara* on October 4, 1980, that said Iraq intended its nuclear facility near Baghdad for use against "the Zionist enemies."

"Despite all the condemnations in the last 24 hours, Israel has nothing to apologize for. It was a just cause. And it shall yet triumph," Begin said. ". . . it was an act of supreme moral and national self-defense."

A student of history, Begin did not want to see himself as the person responsible for failing to take action against something that could end the history of the Jewish race.

His big concern was that an Arab nuclear bomb threat to Israel could spell a final doom for the tiny country and its people.

Two days after Israel's precise destruction of Iraq's nuclear facility at Tammuz, in the audacious and daring raid with dramatic success, Menachem Begin powerfully emphasized his "Never Again" thoughts.

Meanwhile, other Middle East leaders had different ideas about the future of Israel.

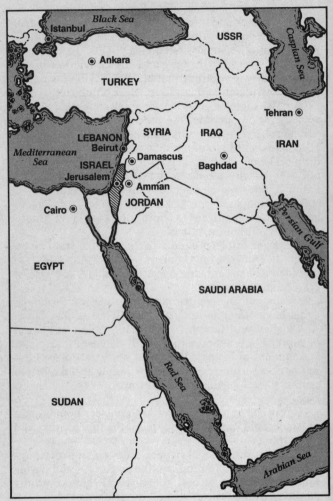

Tiny Israel (stripes) is dwarfed by the Arab countries in the compact Middle East.

Prime Minister Menachem Begin replying to international condemnation of Israel's air strike against Iraq's nuclear reactor. He emphasized his claim that Iraq planned to make at least three atomic bombs at the reactor. (AP/WIDE WORLD PHOTOS)

Military Chief of Staff Lt. General Raphael Eitan, right, shows Prime Minister Menachem Begin the F-16s that took part in the Iraqi raid. Begin visited Ramat David, the home base of the F-16s, to praise the pilots soon after the attack. (AP/Wide World Photos)

F-16 in flight near Massada. Notice lizard-colored paint scheme causes the fighter to blend in easily with desert surroundings.

An Israeli F-16 taxies for take-off.

3

Arrival of the F-16 and Commitment to Training

ONE MAN'S POISON is another man's delight.

The Ayatollah Khomeini's takeover of Iran in January 1979 brought startling changes to the Middle East.

One memorable event occurred November 4, 1979, when 90 U.S. Embassy personnel were taken hostage. They remained captives for 444 days.

A second major event was the jolt of disrupted oil supplies and the alarming escalation of oil prices.

Another less visible result of Khomeini's takeover was the cancellation of the Shah's contract to purchase 160 F-16s from the United States. That cancellation changed combat in the Middle East.

The F-16 had been under development as a new, relatively inexpensive lightweight U.S. fighter to complement the F-15. It went into experimental and engineering production in January 1975 and first flew December 8, 1976.

The small plane was an immediate hit and incorporated some revolutionary concepts. Some of the aircraft parts were constructed with special composites that made it difficult for search and track radars to detect the F-16. It had enormous acceleration, allowing it to climb to 40,000 feet in less than 60 seconds after takeoff roll begins. Its interior design featured new technology for instruments instead of outdated individually monitored instruments.

Computers did in seconds what could not be done at all in other jet fighters to check out all the plane's systems prior to takeoff. It is called BITS—an acronym for Built In Test System. BITS instantly isolates and reduces time and manpower needed to find any problems with the airplane's systems and makes quick repairs possible.

The F-16 features an inertial navigation system (INS) that computes the mission headings, speed and mileage for the pilot with a destination accuracy of one mile radius after a 2,500-mile flight. It is a system similar to the one used by today's commercial airlines. The revolutionary system is internally generated—there is no dependence on outside signals.

The toughest part of using the INS is learning how to punch the correct buttons for the information you want.

The F-16 features a newly designed pilot seat—30-degree tilt-back—so the pilot's heels and fanny are on about the same level. Most planes only have a 13-degree tilt.

The 30-degree tilt allows pilots to pull tighter turns with more gravity (G) force. It makes it tougher for blood to leave the head and go to other parts of the body, which can cause the pilot to black out from pulling or pushing negative G too hard on the control stick.

This slant-back seat that prevents pilot blackout allows the pilot to take advantage of one of the most significant features of the F-16—it has a turn radius one-half that of the F-4 at the same speed and altitude. And its turn radius is better than any known MIG.

In air-to-air combat, this gives the F-16 fighter pilot an advantage over the enemy.

The F-16's maneuverability enables a pilot to shake a tailing enemy plane which is critical in any air-to-air engagement. Since the plane has the ability to out-turn other fighters, the ability of the pilot to survive that tight turn becomes critical. It also allows the pilot to turn inside an enemy aircraft to get on the tail of an enemy aircraft. This is what air-to-air combat is all about. U.S. fighter pilots have to remain in good physical condition to withstand the punishing G forces that can be generated by the F-16.

In fighter planes prior to this development, a pilot could black out around 6 G's or 7 G's, even if his G suit worked properly.

In the F-16, the pilot can stay conscious at 9 G's for a short period of time which gives him a lifesaving advantage.

The newly designed bubble canopy on the F-16 makes it easier than ever for a pilot to get a panoramic view to "check six," that is, to see if there's an enemy plane on his tail.

The pilot almost sits on top of the fuselage instead of inside it so he gets a much better view of his surroundings than pilots in other types of fighters. This advantage is significant in winning and is one of many advantages built into this U.S. fighter.

Another revolutionary design is the pressure-sensitive control stick. For the first time, it's not located between the pilot's legs. It is attached to the right side of the plane and operates the control surfaces through electrical impulses sent to a computer—much like handles at a video arcade. Movement of the stick is measured in sixteenths of an inch compared to the old stick that could be pushed all around the cockpit between the pilot's legs.

It's called FBW, or Fly By Wire, a name given because all signals to the control surfaces are by electrical impulses from the flight computer which receives its commands from the control stick. The plane is dynamically unstable and without this system, it would be uncontrollable in the air.

Pilots at first were alarmed at the unconventional way to control the aircraft, but quickly found it easy to handle.

Because all the important systems are electrical rather than mechanical and hydraulic, the F-16 became nicknamed "The Electric Jet." In Israel, it was called "Falcon" or "Netes," even before the U.S. Air Force made the decision on that name.

The powerful, yet fuel-efficient Pratt & Whitney F-100 engine enables combat operations far beyond anything ever envisioned with the F-4 Phantom. And the F-16 engine is smokeless compared to the F-4, which leaves a long trail of black smoke—making visual spotting of the Phantom by an enemy a dead giveaway.

In Israel, F-4s are smokeless. It was their power and small size that gave the F-16 the edge.

The F-16 with its sophisticated radar fire control system makes dropping bombs easier and more accurate than in any attack plane ever built. Bombs can now be dropped within an average of 15 feet of a target. The F-4 Phantom could not hit consistently within 150 feet of a target.

It has a bomb fall line that is lined up on the target and when the pilot dives toward the target to drop bombs, he keeps this line on the target until a circle at the end of the line called a pipper is on the target. A "death dot" in the middle of the pipper is what the pilot puts the target under.

Then the pilot simply pickles off the bombs—with assurance that if he flies the plane right—the bomb hits with 100 percent accuracy.

For survival during bombing, the F-16 features a sophisticated built-in Radar Warning Receiver (RWR pronounced "raw") that alerts the pilot when an enemy radar is locked onto him. It is in essence an airplane "fuzz buster" that allows the pilot a chance to find those signals and use deceptive tactics to avoid being shot down.

To help the pilot fly the aircraft, especially in a combat situation, a Heads Up Display (HUD) system has been designed and installed.

HUD is simply a system of projecting all the vital instrument information in the cockpit onto a glass window in front of the pilot at eye level. This way, as he looks out of the canopy, the pilot can look at the information reflected on the glass. Now he'll never have to bury his head in the cockpit, even for a second, which could cause him to lose track of the combat situation and risk being shot down.

Information displayed includes G loading, airspeed,

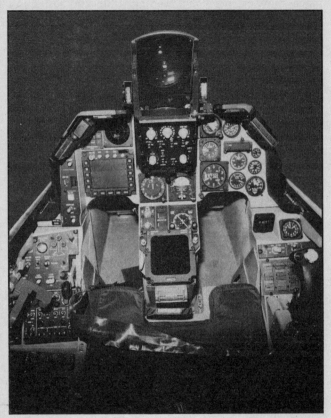

The cockpit of the F-16A flown by the Israelis on the attack. There is no control stick between the pilot's legs. Rather, the fly-by-wire aircraft control handle, similar to that in the space shuttle, is grasped by the pilot's right hand on the right side of the cockpit. The left hand controls the throttle (lower left of picture). The window magnifying type device above the instrument panel is the Heads Up Display (HUD) which shows the pilot all the information on the aircraft and target. Critical flight information is displayed on the TV screen between the pilot's legs and all the armament information is displayed on the digital screen above the pilot's left knee. Above the screen, the clock-like instrument tells the pilot about missiles coming at him.

mach number, magnetic heading, time and miles to destination, altitude and all types of attack symbology depending on whether the pilot wants to shoot the gun, fire air-to-air missiles or drop bombs with pinpoint accuracy.

All in all, the F-16 is a fantastic technological step forward in fighter aircraft.

Iran had purchased 160 F-16s with an envisioned grand total of 350 of the futuristic planes—the largest aircraft order outside the U.S. Air Force. The first planes were to be delivered in 1980.

But the overthrow of the Shah by the Ayatollah Khomeini and his taking hostage of the 65 U.S. diplomats and other embassy personnel canceled the sale and delivery scheduled in 1979.

That left planes on the production line unsold.

Israel had shown interest in the F-16 and made a deal in August 1977 for 75 of the small fighters with scheduled delivery in 1982.

Because of the Shah's downfall, F-16 delivery to Israel started two years earlier than scheduled.

The result was that the Israelis would complete a job for themselves—and the Iranians—a job the Iranians would botch before the Israelis got their chance.

The F-16s were delivered in small lots to Israel through 1980 and 1981.

At the time, there was a shortage of F-16s so the first eight F-16s were delivered to Israel in the United States.

They were used for training Israeli pilots and ground crews in the 388 Tactical Fighter Wing (TFW) and specifically the 16 Tactical Fighter Training Squadron (TFTS) at Hill Air Force Base near Salt Lake City, Utah.

It was there that the pilots were given a three-month course and checkout in the aircraft.

This training included studies in the F-16, its systems, formation flying, performance characteristics, radar use, and how the missile and gun systems worked. The course also included landings, instrument flying, acrobatics, intercepts, Basic Fighter Maneuvers (BFM) of one aircraft fighting another, Air Combat Maneuvering (ACM) when two aircraft fight one, and Air Combat Tactics (ACT) where larger groups of planes fight each other. Also taught were air-to-ground training for Surface Attack bombing (SA) and Surface Attack Tactics (SAT), or how to avoid getting shot down by an enemy employing guns and missiles on the ground or in the air while you're attacking a ground target.

It was a comprehensive course.

They also learned how to be instructor pilots so they could train others in the F-16 once they returned to Israel.

The maintenance ground crews took part in some 40 courses, including electrical systems, weapons repair, and engine and battle damage.

This training allowed Israel's best pilots and ground crewmen to get to know the aircraft during training from expert U.S. pilots and instructors.

The first four planes to go to Israel from the United States were ferried over in July 1980 in an 11-hour, 6,000-mile, nonstop flight with at least three in-flight air refuelings. These were planes that had been used in training.

A total of 53 planes arrived by the time the Iraqi raid took place in 1981.

Without those planes, carrying out a successful strike on the Tammuz reactor would have been very difficult.

Known as Cheyl Ha Avir or Corps of the Air, in Israel, the Israeli Air Force (IAF) is unique among air forces of the world.

Israeli leaders realize air power and control of the skies are vital to the survival of their country. And no air force operates and trains with the intensity of the IAF.

Military service in Israel, with a population of 3.8 million, is compulsory for both men and women when they reach their eighteenth birthday. Men must serve between three and four years, and women, from two to two and a half years of active duty.

After that, they must enter a reserve unit and continue to train an average of one day a month, plus one month a year until the men are 55 and the women 25 years old.

The air force training requirements for reserve pilots are even stricter.

It isn't money that attracts these dedicated people—a colonel makes about $800 a month and a general roughly $1,200 a month. A sergeant gets $400.

Volumes are published on some of the world's great fighter pilots—men like Adolph Galland, Robin Olds, Johnnie Johnson, Pappy Boyington, Eddie Rickenbacker, Oswald Boelcke, Raymond Toliver, Erich Hartmann, Baron Manfred von Richthofen, Randy "Duke" Cunningham and others.

Anywhere fighter pilots or aviation enthusiasts congregate to train, study, or tell stories, the thoughts, doctrines and quotes of these air combat heroes are legend from which all other aspirants draw inspiration.

Yet, because Israel is continuously at war, and because of the brutalities of the Middle East, for protection the identities of their pilots must be kept secret.

It is because of this wartime secrecy that their thoughts and ideas are also restricted knowledge.

As fighter pilot lore goes, it's tragic, because the IAF has about 712 kills in air combat since its inception, which has earned it the reputation as "The World's Best." It has 1,301 kills total by fixed wing aircraft in both the air and on the ground.

All the fighter kills of all the air forces of the world combined since World War II do not equal those of the IAF.

Meanwhile, the Arabs have lost a total of 1,422 aircraft from all causes since 1948.

Size and weaponry of armed forces are only two aspects of a nation's military strength.

There are other components: the skill, courage, ingenuity and daring used when bringing those military forces into play. These are incalculable factors and sometimes can outweigh sheer size.

What nuggets of wisdom are enthusiasts denied because of this continuing war? But conversely, those same nuggets of inspiration and knowledge work for the benefit of the IAF.

There is a serious yet businesslike atmosphere among air force personnel.

The relationship between officers and enlisted men is accepted, yet there are not the stuffy demands on discipline, procedural issues and saluting found in other air forces.

The basic philosophy of this elite force is getting the job done. Training is so demanding and rigorous that little time is left to worry about discretionary relationships like military courtesies.

It very much resembles an air force under wartime conditions—which it is—24 hours a day, 365 days a year. Work days are routinely 12 hours, from 7:00 A.M. to 7:00 P.M., five and a half days a week during periods of normal crisis and six or seven when events require.

There are tough demands that make family life difficult.

War among most nations and combatants generally lasts a few years, maybe as long as five or six. Somehow the conflicts generally end and the troops get a rest from the tensions and pressures of war.

In Israel, it has been a lifetime of war—which gives enormous advantage in experience, but also pressures that can wear down a person. So far, the IAF has adopted to the pressure.

Ask an Israeli fighter pilot, "Do you think there will be war soon in the Middle East?"

His simple answer, "There is no need to talk about it, only prepare for it."

Most bases are in remote areas, which makes going to the big city a major event. Maintenance on aircraft is continuous. Ground crews never go home until all aircraft for which they are responsible are completely flyable and operational—even if it takes all night to get them in that condition. Every morning, with the exception of a few planes going through major overhaul, all the combat planes of the entire IAF are ready for war. It's like being on constant alert.

Flight training is given at Hatzerim Air Base in southern Israel. Most students start at the age of 18 or 19, not after having earned college degrees as in the U.S. Air Force. The training is so tough that only two in ten who enter ever graduate.

Those who do graduate are scaled and graded in a way that only the very cream of the cream are selected for fighters. The pilots can have a choice of what they want to fly, but unlike many other air forces in the world, their record of flying skills and attitude in training determines their future—not politics or quotas.

Generally, all pilots go directly to an active duty A-4 Skyhawk attack or bombing squadron right out of school where they learn first-hand the operational lessons of the IAF.

To keep morale up and cross-talk or exchange ideas with the new IAF student pilots, usually each of the recent graduates returns to his training unit to fly with the new pilots in training. This could be as often as once a week.

However, since 1980, there has been an effort to selectively place exceptionally qualified pilots directly into high-performing squadrons such as the F-16, F-15, or KFIR.

There has not yet been a true "nugget" or direct flight school graduate brought into the front seat of the F-4 without first operationally flying another jet. This is due to the difficulty of flying it and the complexity of its Israeli-unique integrated weapon system.

Great responsibility is placed on youth. Squadron commanders are in their early thirties. By contrast, in the U.S. Navy or Air Force, the average age for squadron commander is 40. Since the IAF was established in November 1947 (which included the pre-independence Air Service, a division of the Haganah), IAF commanders' average age has been 42 when they took command.

It operates from ten main bases scattered throughout Israel. They are well hidden, protected and camouflaged. Most fighter and attack aircraft are parked, stored and protected in giant underground hangars, but dummy aircraft are scattered around the field as decoys. On the ground, there is extremely tight, and if necessary, deadly security.

The air force is structured for maximum training flights to keep experience levels high and proficiency at a peak. All pilots fly to keep their performance levels in a state of wartime readiness, even when they are stationed at a desk in the headquarters, or are in the reserves. There is no time to allow for training once a war starts.

After serving as a squadron commander, selected pilots go up the totem pole and eventually become wing/base commanders. These are men who have proven themselves in combat and are considered excellent pilots. Usually they are capable of flying all the aircraft stationed on the base under their command, but generally just stay proficient in the type of fighter in which they have the most experience.

Unlike U.S. Navy and Air Force wing commanders, the Israeli wing commander is in direct command of everything on his base, from the plumbers and chow lines to the planes and pilots. He is king.

As the date for delivering the first F-16s approached, the high command of the IAF determined who would be the men selected to fly the planes, who would be the first two squadron commanders and where the planes would be based.

The top pilots were picked, and little did anyone realize they were destined to leave their mark on the pages of history—publicly.

Dov was selected as the first F-16 squadron commander and he had had a previous command as commanding officer (CO) of an F-4 squadron. Dan was picked to command the second F-16 squadron. It was his first command. He also was a highly skilled F-4 Phantom pilot. Both men were combat-proven veterans. The IAF commander wanted experience to ensure that the new squadron of expensive planes would have the highest levels of experience.

Dov was a 32-year-old lieutenant colonel at the time and a MIG killer. He was a soft-spoken, slender man of medium height, with close-cropped black hair and a warm smile that radiated from green eyes. The father of four, he had a great interest in history and a gentle dedication to his family. He was a man who inspired confidence.

The CO of the second squadron was Dan, a 35-year-old lieutenant colonel, father of two, and the second-highest scoring jet fighter pilot of all time from any air force in the world. (The number one worldwide jet ace is also an Israeli.) He demanded total dedication and long hours of his men and himself.

Dan, short, skinny, and already with gray specks in his short brown hair, was full of boundless enthusiasm and energy.

Dan was awarded the OT HAOZ, the IAF's second-highest award for courage on the field of battle for his actions during the 1973 Yom Kippur War. At the time, he and another pilot had intuitive feelings they were about to suffer a surprise attack by Egyptian MIGs on their remote base at Ophir near Sharmel-Sheikh at the southern end of the Sinai.

When that feeling hit Dan, both pilots and their back-seat weapon systems officers jumped into their F-4 Phantoms and scrambled in the air just seconds before Egyptian MIGs pounded the airfield with 500-pound bombs. The two Israeli pilots took on 12 Egyptian MIGs and between the two of them blasted seven out of the sky. Neither of their planes was damaged.

The badly mauled Egyptians never returned to attack that base during the remainder of the war.

Dan was older than Dov, but held the same rank because he first served as a tank commander in the army before he could talk his way into the air force. After graduation from flight school, he was plowed back as an instructor pilot, much to his displeasure. It took him two years of fighting the air force to get into fighters.

Besides being a fighter ace, Dan qualified for the Israeli Olympic rifle team. He was also an excellent race car driver, an accomplished artist and a computer whiz.

Dov was the first to go to Utah for F-16 training in February 1980. Three other pilots went with him, including Joseph and Amos.

Dan led the second contingent starting in April 1980.

Samuel took the third group of four to Hill Air Force Base in July 1980.

Simultaneously, high-level discussions were going on at IAF Headquarters about what to do if it became necessary to attack the Iraqi nuclear reactor by air. If it were to be attacked, which plane or planes would be used? There were arguments and counterarguments.

The single-seat, single-engine A-4 Skyhawk and Israeli-built KFIR's were the country's primary attack aircraft. But neither had the range or the sophisticated radar and bomb-sight equipment. They were eliminated from consideration. That left the F-4 Phantoms, the F-15, and the soon-to-arrive F-16.

The F-4 was a serious contender, but it had its drawbacks. It was a large, heavy brute of an aircraft, lacked maneuverability, guzzled fuel and couldn't carry enough fuel to make the round trip without in-flight refueling. It also had a two-man crew which meant double the number of men killed or captured for every aircraft lost on the raid.

It was a good 20-year-old veteran, and its constant modernization made it a contender until the final decision was made, especially if precision-guided missiles (PGMs) were used. That is, bombs guided to the target by devices in the plane.

When slick bombs were selected—the F-4 was out. That left a real debate. Should it be the F-15 or the F-16?

The F-15 had been in the Israeli inventory since 1977. It was primarily designed as an air-to-air fighter, held the world altitude climb speed records, possessed a look-down shoot-down pulse Doppler radar capability of locking targets flying at altitudes as low as 20 feet above the ground and yet was able to discriminate them from ground clutter. With a lock-on-target range in excess of 100 miles, it truly has the best fire control system in existence.

It is a big airplane with twin engine reliability with two of the earlier model Pratt & Whitney F-100 engines that

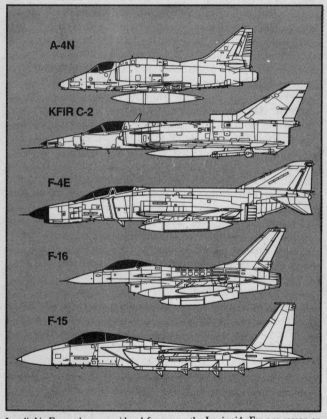

A-4N

KFIR C-2

F-4E

F-16

F-15

Israeli Air Force planes considered for use on the Iraqi raid. For one reason or another, all planes were rejected except the F-16.

powered the single engine F-16. But those F-15 engines didn't perform with the reliability demanded by the IAF. Modifications were made later. There was worry whether the F-15s could all safely fly to Baghdad and back.

The F-15 has a centerline and two wing tanks for carrying external fuel. But it also has specially designed conformal or fast-pack fuel tanks that can be bolted to the side of the engines. They are aerodynamically designed to avoid much increase in drag or lack of maneuverability. They virtually double the amount of fuel the plane can carry and the range it can fly. That is, they add about 1,000 miles of high altitude flying. But they can't be dropped once the plane is engaged in combat.

IAF officials found that one key problem with using the F-15 was the conformal or fuselage-hugging fuel tanks—the IAF couldn't get its hands on any. By not selling any of these special tanks to Israel, the United States was trying to keep its Air Force on a short tether. Eventually, Israel would have to build its own.

Discussion continued and a decision was finally made.

If the political leadership of Israel wanted to bomb the Iraqi reactor, it would be with the small, hard-to-detect, hard-to-hit, maneuverable F-16 and its pinpoint bombing accuracy. It was the only plane that could carry the heavy 2,000-pound MK84 bombs to the target without air-to-air refueling.

When Dov returned from his training at Hill AFB, he had been expecting to increase his MIG kill count, especially against the Syrians, with the maneuverable F-16. The last thought on his mind was dropping bombs.

When he returned to Israel, Gen. David Ivri, Chief of Staff of the IAF called Dov to his office for a polite talk about the plane's capabilities and a description of his training in Utah. Then to his astonishment, Ivri ordered him to commence low-level navigation training of his squadron for a bombing mission at the farthest range the plane was capable of flying.

4

The Terror of the Tigris

THE MIDDLE EAST is full of emotional, hate-filled leaders who have expressed ugly enmity toward Israel—Assad of Syria, Khomeini of Iran, Moammar Gadhafi of Libya.

But none is more brutal, savage, ruthless, cruel, power-hungry, possessed with distrust and lack of loyalty, nor has displayed a more bloody climb to the top than the strongman dictator or Iraq—where the ends justify the means—"The Butcher of Baghdad"—"The Terror of the Tigris"—Saddam Hussein.

The mention of two subjects will ignite Hussein into a rage quicker than a snap of the fingers—Iran and Israel.

And not necessarily in that order.

The subjects also include Israel's main supporter as well—the United States.

Iraq has been at war with Israel since 1948 when the original war of independence for Israel was won.

Iraq has never made peace or even agreed to a cease-fire with Israel after the 1948 war, the 1967 war or the 1973 war.

It has participated in all the wars, but simply faded away once the fighting stopped—with a mind set to destroy Israel at the next opportunity.

As far as Iraq is concerned, a state of war still exists with Israel.

Even Syria, Jordan and Egypt have at least agreed to

26

cease-fires, and in the 1978 Camp David Accords, Egypt recognized Israel's right to exist as a country in a controversial peace treaty that evoked the enmity of the Arab world.

One of Iraq's chief impediments in its attempt to destroy Israel is distance. Baghdad sits 600 miles from tiny Israel, which is buffered by Saudi Arabia, Jordan and Syria, all of which also share a common border with Iraq.

Iraq has two of the most famous rivers of history running parallel and bisecting the country from the northwest to the south—the Euphrates and the Tigris.

In the middle of the country they come within 20 miles of each other—and it's at this point on the Tigris River that Baghdad is located.

Its location is a little more than 100 miles north of the site of the ancient city of Babylon which was leveled in about 130 B.C.

Aside from the rich valleys of the river areas, Iraq is an isolated desert area with 13 million people. In 1980, oil revenues from Iraq's chief export were $25 billion. They fell to $6.7 billion in 1982, mostly as a result of the conflict with Iran. The war is costing Iraq an estimated $1 billion a month.

Iraq has a gross national product (GNP) of $18 billion and, until the war with Iran blossomed, spent about 20 percent of its GNP on defense—$3.5 billion annually.

At the start of the Iran-Iraq war the army consisted of 190,000 troops comprising 12 divisions—four armored and two mechanized.

The army had 2,200 tanks including 1,000 state-of-the-art Russian T-62s, 1,700 artillery pieces and a variety of missiles.

The air force consisted of 30,000 troops and 450 attack aircraft including 140 MIG 23, Flogger E's, SU-17 Fitter C and SU-20 Fitter H and TU-22 Blinder medium bombers, plus 225 helicopters, some of them U.S. made.

The navy had 4,000 sailors, 12 torpedo boats, 14 anti-missile boats plus 19 other types of boats.

Iraqi President Saddam Hussein. (UPI/Bettmann Newsphotos)

Because of the Iran-Iraq war, Iraqi military growth and modernization has been enormous. The size of the army has tripled. The air force has expanded from more than 400 tactical jets to more than 600. A formidable force for such a small country.

They also possessed the desire and commitment to build a nuclear bomb.

Hussein's climb to leadership in Iraq left a trail of bloody bodies, tricky maneuvering and a growth of commitment that even terrifies terrorists.

The background of this man who is so possessed and driven would be a challenge for a novelist to create.

Born in 1937 on the outskirts of Takrit, 100 miles north of Baghdad, life has been one continuous scheming struggle for Hussein.

His father, an ordinary farmer, died before he was born and Hussein was raised by a powerful, domineering maternal uncle, Khairallah Tulfah.

Tulfah had children of his own and for Hussein to survive, he was forced to fight for attention and status in the foster family.

He learned to take nothing for granted. To fight for everything.

He realized to achieve anything he'd have to win it himself and thus became fiercely independent.

This training prepared him to survive and achieve in the brutal jungle of Iraqi politics. In such an environment he honed his political skills—yet created a distrust for his fellow man that haunts him to this day.

Tulfah is credited with shaping much of Hussein's personality. It's believed Hussein patterned his slightly theatrical mannerisms—his slow deliberate movements that are calculated to create an air of authority—after Tulfah.

His mother later married his dead father's brother—Ibrahim al-Hassan al-Takrit—and the family moved to the city of Kirkuk, 75 miles northwest of his rural childhood home.

Hussein was still a youngster, but was now part of a

new family of brothers and sisters. He was the eldest, and as Arab tradition goes, he received special privileges. His brothers were subordinate to his wishes and were expected to cater to his every whim.

But to balance it off, he felt a strong sense of responsibility for them.

Hussein adopted a similar outlook as president of Iraq.

He expects all his followers to kowtow to him and to automatically respect him. He rewards this subservience by his efforts to make Iraq the leader of the Arab world—regardless of the cost.

The family shifted cities again when Hussein was ten years old—moving back to Takrit—where he started his schooling. Saddam Hussein earned his reputation for cruelty and callousness at an early age. During this school period in Takrit it is believed he committed his first murders.

He is reputed to have murdered a man in the course of an inter-clan dispute. He also is said to have murdered the head of the local Communist Party—an official named Sa'adun al-Takriti.

In 1955, he went to Baghdad for his high school education at the al Karkh school—a center of the growing student nationalist movement against the British supported rule of King Faisal II.

His Uncle Khairallah lived there and provided housing for the 18-year-old student.

Entering high school at 18 was not unusual for young men who wanted to evade the draft. Hussein never served in the army.

While going to school in Baghdad he joined the Ba'ath political party and knifed his way to power. Why he joined that party is a mystery. It only had 300 members and had relatively no influence. Some feel it was the ideology of the party as much as anything that captured his interest.

Established in 1940 by French-educated intellectuals led by the Syrian philosopher Michel Aflak, the Ba'ath (Arabic for resurrection) Party dreamed of a united, secular socialist Arab nation. Western belief in progress was interwoven with the ideal of Arab nationhood.

The party slogan—"Unity, Freedom and Socialism" —inspired thousands of educated Arabs who were not particularly enthralled with Islam.

His character of ruthlessness, brutality and cunning evolved during those years.

In 1956, Hussein was a key ingredient in the anti-monarchial underground. With several accomplices from the Ba'ath Party, he was arrested and put in prison for several months for attempting to overthrow the government. That experience only set in concrete his conviction and beliefs in the Ba'ath Party.

King Faisal was killed in 1958 in a coup headed by Gen. Abdel Karim Kassem who became Iraq's new strongman.

Three years later, on October 7, 1959, Hussein was part of a ten-man commando unit that set out to assassinate General Kassem.

The group stepped out into one of Baghdad's main streets and sprayed the dictator's station wagon with gunfire but failed to kill him. Hussein was wounded in the leg by a poorly aimed shot from one of his fellow conspirators but dragged himself away from the scene before authorities found him. Alone, he pulled out his commando knife, dug into his leg and pulled out the bullet—all without anesthetic.

He made his way back to his hometown of Takrit. A wanted man, the Ba'ath smuggled him across the desert on a donkey for the harsh and dangerous trip to asylum in Damascus. He received a hero's welcome as the only revolutionary to successfully escape.

Stories of his toughness and bravery preceded him and the top leaders of the Syrian Ba'ath greeted him on his arrival. The leader of the party, Michel Aflak, personally swore him into the Ba'ath Party. This saga has been immortalized in an Iraqi novel and film presented as national heroic theater.

At 22, Hussein was standing tall among the party's

chosen and a close bond formed between him and Aflak, the Ba'ath's unquestioned ideological leader. That bond would serve Hussein well in coming years.

Meanwhile, in Baghdad, Hussein was sentenced to death in absentia.

After a year in Damascus, Egyptian President Gamal Abdel Nasser heard of his exploits and had him move to Cairo where he kept up his activities in the Ba'ath Party. While there, Hussein attempted to complete high school and studied law. But his trail of cruelty continued. He was arrested for having allegedly murdered a compatriot, Mamduh-al-Alus, who had been his teacher and was released after the personal intervention of President Nasser.

For the next two years, Hussein maintained a low profile in Egypt, but managed to rise to the leadership of the Cairo cell of the Ba'ath Party. It was during this stay in Egypt that he began the underground life of plotting and organizing that would bring him to power. However he developed no loyalty to those who sheltered him either in Egypt or Syria.

In 1963, the Ba'ath Party staged a takeover in Iraq. Hussein returned to Baghdad and used the prevailing anarchy to develop his own place in the Ba'ath Party. While political rivals were busy killing each other, he built a tight nucleus of followers loyal only to him.

Despite his youth, he appeared to be a pillar of stability in the madness which engulfed post-revolutionary Iraq—solidifying his position as leader. But the Ba'ath's hold over Iraq was far from stable, and within a year Hussein had to go underground.

His hiding place was discovered in October of 1964 and a fierce gun battle with an overwhelming force of police assaulting his hideout followed. He fought them off until he ran out of bullets.

Saddam was arrested and jailed for the next 21 months. But in July 1966, while being taken to court for trial, he managed to escape and went underground again.

In December 1966, when his political archrival Abdur-

Rahman Aref was killed in a helicopter crash, Hussein received a pardon. He stayed in the shadows another year and a half—consolidating his power in the Ba'ath Party. During this time he continued to plot the revolution which shook Iraq on July 17, 1968. It was a successful bloodless coup largely due to the party militia Hussein organized.

Although the revolution was Hussein's brainchild, Ahmed Hassan-al-Bakr became president and was deeply grateful to his young protégé. So grateful in fact, that Bakr was happy to confine himself to the symbolic duties of the presidency and leave Hussein to run the country as vice president. With Bakr's blind consent, Hussein systematically swept away even the slightest hint of opposition. He had the full support and cooperation of Iraq's zealous secret service in achieving his goals.

His ruthlessness surfaced again.

Within two weeks, he had organized another revolt that was a trap. This time, he invited the head of the main opposition party with the newly formed coalition to lunch. Nayef Daoud was instantly arrested and packed off to London with a clear warning: "Return to Iraq and you're dead."

Shortly after taking office Hussein announced that he had discovered a plot against him. He had about 30 leading Ba'ath members killed, including five members of the ruling Revolutionary Command Council. One of the victims had been one of his closest companions in the struggle for power, Abdel Khalik al-Samuri. Another was the dreaded national director of security, Col. Hazem Kazzar.

And so it went.

One former colleague after another was neutralized by a complicated process of intrigue and back-stabbing. No holds were barred and nothing was allowed to get in Hussein's way. On November 10, 1969, a special law was passed naming him vice president and deputy chairman of the Revolutionary Council of the Ba'ath Party. From there he appointed his revolutionary colleagues into positions of little authority while he kept all the power. He designed the Ba'ath Party so it controlled everything, with the ultimate goal of ruling the Arab world.

The party's hold on power is protected by a machine which appears to be as pervasive, rigidly organized and ideologically committed as Russia's Communist Party. Every government department head is a party person. Every army unit has a party political officer. Every military academy cadet is a member. Every school, university and neighborhood has its party cells. Every member of the 500,000-strong popular army, a militia that augments the regular army, is a card-carrying member.

This feat of political organization has been accomplished in the 16 years since President Hussein seized power.

In 1968, the party could count on only a few hundred men who had operated underground for a decade. Today, it is said to have in excess of 1.25 million members in a population of 13 million.

Party membership is an exclusive privilege with elaborate rituals. "To become a member can take ten years. Once a member, you can never leave—except maybe in a coffin," said a dissident Iraqi journalist in London.

Candidates attend weekly indoctrination meetings where they are carefully observed. They read extensively in the party's literature and discuss socialism and Arab nationalism. Eventually, they are assigned tasks ranging from messenger work to spending the summer teaching villagers to read and write. Watching and informing on antiparty elements is also an assignment.

The party demands ideological purity, total obedience, absolute loyalty.

Initially designated as a naseer, or supporter, a recruit joins a party cell of three to seven members. Chiefs of five to seven cells form the next level of the power pyramid, a grand cell or firqa. A collection of grand cells makes up a branch.

Messages from the base are communicated promptly to the top of the pyramid, the party's Regional Command, and above that to the Revolutionary Command Council headed by President Hussein. He is also secretary general of the Regional Command and Supreme Commander of the armed forces.

The men and women who run the party believe they are the guardians of the Arab world's most progressive, humane ideal and are loyal to their leader. Members accept the party as supreme, above family and friends. The Ba'ath is ruthless when dealing with its own. Not even family bonds are sacred for Hussein.

In January 1969, an Iraqi merchant and personal friend of his Uncle Khairallah, Abdul Hamid-a-Damarji, was accused of plotting against the government. He was outside Iraq at the time and could not be arrested.

Years later, Khairallah asked Hussein to reprieve a-Damarji and allow him to return to Iraq, as a personal favor for the man who partly raised Hussein. Hussein agreed.

But the moment a-Damarji arrived in Iraq, he was arrested. Khairallah was shattered at the broken promise. He quit all high posts he had been given and returned to the seclusion of his farm in Takrit. Vengeance clearly took place over family loyalty in Hussein's priorities of life.

By the time he entered leadership, Saddam Hussein was ideally equipped to dominate those he controlled.

Fiercely independent, a loner who trusted no one and felt beholden to no one, he was prepared and able to trample on anyone who stood in his way. He had all the cunning and courage of the loner and was adept in the art of manipulating his fellow man to attain his goals. His rise through the ranks of power in Iraq is a chronicle of infighting, murder, Machiavellian intrigue, and ruthlessness.

His cruelty knew no bounds when it came to settling accounts with his political rivals. He eliminated them either by brute force or by deception—or by kicking them upstairs to positions in which they could retain their privileges but have no say in affairs of state.

He surrounded himself with men whose allegiance was fortified by fear and their loyalty was assured by a network of informants.

Hussein's period as the number two man in the Iraqi hierarchy was insurance of a stable country—even at the cost of much blood. One of the main problems facing his new regime was the Kurdish revolt along the northern border of Iraq. Hussein set this problem high on his list of priorities.

He signed an agreement with Kurdish leader Mustafa Barazani on March 11, 1970, promising the Kurds full autonomy within four years. In what appeared to be a conciliatory move, Hussein gave in to all the demands of the Kurds, who were surprised but happy to accept the peace arrangement. Peace was brought to the country's northern frontier.

When he was in a better position to deal effectively with the problem four years later, Hussein reneged on every promise to the Kurds and the war was renewed in 1974.

His word of honor was meaningless.

Hussein learned an important lesson from his manipulation of the Kurds. He put it to practice on the Shah of Iran.

He made a deal with the Shah—Iran could have the much-fought-over Shatt al-Arab on condition that Iran stop supporting the Kurds.

The Shah honored his commitment which allowed Hussein to then fight effectively against the Kurds and have a single front on which to fight. Thinking his army could strike lightning fast and believing his own publicity, Hussein pulled a double-cross and declared war on Iran in September 1980, to regain by force what he had given up in a tactical move so he could quiet Kurd opposition five years earlier.

It was typical Hussein, but so far his army has been unable to deliver because of inept leadership.

In order to achieve his ultimate goal, Hussein will stop at nothing. A master strategist and a tactical manipulator, Hussein knows exactly what he wants to achieve, no matter what the short-term implications.

In 1972, he signed a mutual assistance and friendship pact with the Soviets which enabled him to nationalize his country's oil industry and gradually enlarge his army from five to 12 divisions, and in the bargain give his troops the best arms the West and East could offer.

And at the same time, he made his initial contacts to acquire nuclear capability.

In 1978, at a time when he was not yet president but was in all respects running the country, Hussein opened a campaign against Iraqi Communists.

Twenty-one Communists in the military were executed by firing squad in June and several thousand were arrested. The executioners were brought from all parts of the country. In effect it was a blood pact among party members from throughout the country to ensure their power.

The fact that the Soviets were Iraq's biggest arms supplier didn't deter Hussein, although it did cause some strains in Iraq's relations with Moscow. But that relationship runs hot and cold depending upon the Soviets' goals as well as Hussein's.

As cunning as he is, Hussein figures he can get away with his desires and actions with the Soviets, since they always cater to unrest. He knows he is a good tool to serve Soviet interests to export trouble—when it serves his interests as well.

But Hussein also had to convey the image of a man involved in politics for the good of his country and not for his personal advantage. So in July 1979, he tired of playing second fiddle as vice president, although he was pulling all the levers of power, and President Bakr, claiming health problems, resigned.

The general feeling is that they were genuine health problems—resign if he wanted to stay healthy enough to stay alive.

Reportedly, Bakr was then placed under house arrest. Some reports said that he had been murdered, but they have never been verified and it's assumed that he's still alive.

Coming to power, Hussein began to promote himself throughout the land to get recognition.

A stocky man with a bristling mustache, thick, bushy coal-black eyebrows, Hussein married a first cousin, Sajida Khairallah Talfah in 1963. They had two sons and two daughters.

He has an impressive appearance—well-groomed, and deliberate in his movements and speech—which reinforces his image as a leader.

He went out of his way to develop a personality cult reminiscent of Stalin in the Soviet Union. He appeared daily on state television, greeting visitors, talking with children and exhorting troops and distributing modern goods made possible by oil wealth. Vocal groups appear on TV most evenings to sing rhythmic ditties praising his prowess.

His portrait hangs everywhere: on posters plastered on lamp posts, bus stations, store windows, air terminals, on the walls of buildings, in restaurants and hotel lobbies, and outside mosques. Twelve-foot-high cutouts stand before some ministries.

Soon after taking office, he changed from a suit with broad pin stripes to a more Third World style, wearing a red checkered Arab scarf on his head.

Since the war with Iran started, he has been appearing in uniform with a field marshall's insignia although he never served in the armed forces. He has also awarded himself many military and academic medals and distinctions.

His iron-fisted rule commands respect mainly by the fear he arouses and his demonstrated control of the sources of power in Iraq. To control dissent and communication, no Iraqi is allowed to own a typewriter without a license.

His ruthlessness is legend. Amnesty International, the human rights organization, says it has the names of 520 political prisoners reported to have been executed in Iraq between 1978 and 1983 and the names of 23 people said to have died while undergoing torture during that same period.

Iraq has always been one of Israel's most implacable foes. But Hussein recognizes that the destruction of Israel should not be an immediate Arab goal, but only the end result of a long process of Arab consolidation under the leadership of a powerful Iraq.

In 1973, he became optimistic when it looked like Syria was going to regain the Golan Heights from Israel. He sent three Iraqi divisions to the Syrian front. However, the tide of battle turned and the troops had to come home.

Any talk of Arab peace with Israel is repulsive to Hussein. He put together the Baghdad Summit Conference in October 1978 to coordinate the Arab world's position on the Israeli-Egyptian peace treaty. Naturally, Iraq's position was the hardest core of all against the "Zionist Imperialists" and Sadat the "traitor."

When Egyptian President el-Anwar Sadat began negotiations with Israel, Hussein saw his chance to take command of the loosely knit opposition to peace with Israel.

Exercising strong leadership against Israel after the Camp David Accords were signed in September 1978, Iraq invited Arab heads of state to Baghdad to take "the necessary steps" to oppose the agreement of peace between fellow Arabs, the Egyptians, and Israel.

Hussein managed to unite hardline, moderate and easy-going Arabs into a single position of rejection of the Camp David Accords and punishment of Egypt, should it go ahead with a separate peace treaty. He also kept King Hussein of Jordan away from the process—a most notable feat.

In a follow-up meeting after the peace treaty in March, Iraq won a consensus of 18 Arab delegations on economic and political sanctions against Cairo.

If they couldn't get rid of Israel, the Arabs were bound and determined to punish any "brothers" who weren't die-hard opponents of the Jews.

The anti-Sadat campaign projected Hussein into an Arab leadership position with little cost.

Iraq had little trade with Egypt and no substantial investments there. It depended upon Egyptian migrant labor, but the Baghdad Agreement excluded "the Egyptian people" from sanctions.

He set out again to build Iraq into a powerful political, economic and military force. Boldly attacking and grievously damaging or destroying Israel would instantly catapult Hussein to leadership of the Arab world and secure for him hero status in the annals of Islam. He would have accomplished at a single stroke what massed Arab armies had been unable to achieve in 30 years of assault and defeat.

In 1978, there were public rumors of Israel's possession of nuclear weapons. From then on, Hussein became convinced he needed nuclear weapons to defeat Israel.

He had taken a close personal interest in Iraq's nuclear program as the critical ingredient needed to destroy Israel and allow Iraq to inherit its right as the most powerful Arab country and leader of the Arab world. But he was in competition for the honor with Moammar Gadhafi, dictator of Libya, who was also in the pursuit of nuclear capability.

Hussein had always been careful prior to the Israeli raid to stress the peaceful aims of the Iraq nuclear program.

But he did slip once. In September 1975, he was quoted as saying Iraq's acquisition of nuclear technology was "the first attempt toward nuclear arming—although the officially declared purpose of the construction of a reactor was not nuclear weapons."

Israel reportedly had nuclear weapons it had manufactured.

The Terror of the Tigris and the Iron Man of Baghdad definitely had set a course to use whatever means it took to equal the rumors of Israel's nuclear might. Israel believed his past actions left no question that he would not hesitate to use nuclear weapons to destroy Israel.

5

Mushrooms in the Desert or Bomb, Bomb, Who's Got the Bomb?

WAS ARAB AGGRESSIVENESS and the threat to Israel's security and future severe enough for the tiny Jewish state to develop nuclear weapons?

During the late 1950s and early 1960s a debate raged in the leadership halls of government.

Despite some stunning conventional military victories in the 1948 War of Independence and the Sinai in 1956, Israel has never felt secure about its future. Leaders have always been concerned over threats from their surrounding Arab enemies. Would they always have a secure source for weapons and weapon systems in times of conflict? Would allies always remain allies? Could changes in foreign governments close off needed defensive military support and leave Israel vulnerable? Would the Soviets supply more technologically advanced conventional weapons to the Arabs? Could an Arab state join the nuclear club? If so, without Israel's retaliatory ability, could the nation of Israel survive?

The Suez operation was to answer many of these questions.

When the Soviet Union and the United States successfully put the pressure on the French and British to stop their Suez adventure, Prime Minister Ben Gurion realized Israel could depend on no one for its survival.

Powerful as they were, the British and French were no

longer able to act independently of the United States and the Soviet Union in the Middle East.

At this point, Ben Gurion knew Israel had to take the necessary steps to ensure his country's future without depending on allies. He recognized that the animosity of the Arabs toward Israel would be a long-term problem.

Ben Gurion huddled with close advisers, including his deputy Shimon Péres and Gen. Moshe Dayan, Chief of Staff of the Israeli Defense Forces. Both men were later to become key players in Israel's political and military scene.

The three discussed the continuing threats to Israel, particularly in view of its small size in territory and population. They felt the potential to be an outcast in the Middle East forced Israel to develop the best weapons possible—including nuclear.

It was a monumental decision—and they vowed to keep it a closely guarded secret. Even most Cabinet members were kept ignorant of the decision.

It was mid-1957. Who could help Israel become a nuclear power? At that point, the only close ally Israel had was France. In October 1957, a deal was struck with the French to help Israel gain nuclear knowledge. It was negotiated by Shimon Péres.

Immediately, hundreds of engineers, research scientists and technicians set up nuclear research facilities in Dimona, a town in the isolated Negev Desert whose nearest neighbor was the city of Beersheba. Construction on the facility started in total secrecy and proceeded that way until 1960—with one exception.

In March 1958, a United States high-altitude top secret U-2 spy plane flying above 70,000 feet photographed the Dimona site with sophisticated equipment and cameras. The CIA soon learned about the project.

The Israelis tried to intercept the plane with Mystere IV and Super Mystere BII fighters—the best planes they possessed. But they couldn't get high enough. They just helplessly watched U.S. intelligence learn what they were trying to hide.

Ben Gurion's fears of unreliable allies were realized in 1960 with the change in the French government. Charles De Gaulle established the Fifth Republic and in mid-May the Israelis were notified the uranium promised for their nuclear research facility would not be delivered.

Not only that, the French insisted Israel must publicly acknowledge their nuclear research at Dimona, since De Gaulle wanted to improve his relations with the Arabs.

In mid-June, Ben Gurion made an official visit to France. He was grudgingly forced to agree to publicly announce construction of the Dimona nuclear facility and that it was being built for peaceful purposes.

In addition, he had to assure the French that Israel did not intend to produce nuclear weapons and that they would not build a separation plant for plutonium. In return, the French promised to provide Israel all the remaining parts they needed to complete the reactor.

This presented Ben Gurion a new set of problems—chief among them was where he would get the uranium to get the research facility operational.

"Never mind, let's get it built. We'll worry about that later," was his reaction.

It's obvious the French didn't believe the Israeli promises and they leaked the information about Dimona to the United States as pressure to ensure that Israel went public. The United States played ignorant, of course. It was already aware of the project because of the U-2 flights.

One last push to put Israel on the spot and assure the project became public: the French leaked it to the press.

On December 16, 1960, the *Daily Express* in London had banner headlines telling that Israel was working on nuclear weapons. On December 18, the *Washington Post* reported the Israelis would be able to produce nuclear weapons within five years. That same day, the *New York Times* announced the French were involved with Israel.

Ben Gurion was stunned and deeply hurt. He had failed in his efforts to keep the project secret.

But the French actions proved to him he was correct in doing everything to ensure a powerful Israel. Friends could turn on you. You could count on no one except yourself.

Charles De Gaulle made a statement in which Ben Gurion now believed: "Treaties are like roses and young girls. They last while they last."

The 1967 war and Israel's smashing victory provided many lessons and reiterated some old ones. The Arabs could always count on arms from the Soviet Union. But Israel's fortunes with free world support would ebb and flow like the tide. For example, immediately after the war, the French embargoed the sale of conventional arms to Israel and the British banned sale of their Chieftain tanks. The United States also put strict conditions on the use of weapons they sold.

Experience of the 1967 war proved to Moshe Dayan, the defense minister at the time, that Israel was too dependent for its security on foreign powers.

The French embargo on conventional arms to Israel immediately after the war and the refusal of the British government to sell Chieftain tanks to Israel proved to be too risky from Dayan's point of view. According to his logic, Israel could independently achieve most of the means to secure its future. Thus, in Dayan's days at the Defense Ministry, the decision was reached to build independent Israeli weapon systems so the country could become self-sufficient in weapon development. This included the fighter-bomber KFIR and the new Israeli main battle tank, the Merkava. Such means as these could secure the Jewish state's future, as long as only the Arabs were involved in the conflict.

But Dayan was mainly concerned about the Soviet Union. Since Russian support for the Arabs had been guaranteed for many long years, the same could hardly be said about United States support for Israel.

In order to improve its diplomatic capability and to

secure those territories which it believed necessary for defense, Israel had to create uncertainty over Russian readiness in order to become directly involved in the conflict. Israel needed to deter the USSR.

The war of attrition along the Suez Canal, the acts of Palestinian terrorism within the Israeli borders and abroad, as well as preparations made by other Arab armies for a war against Israel, all contributed to Dayan's fears.

But more than anything else, Dayan was frightened by the possibility that in the long run, Israel would not be able to afford a new conventional arms race in the Middle East. Although Israel's victory in 1967 was absolute, the Arabs did not show any sign that they were ready to enter negotiations.

In fighting the wars of attrition along its borders, Israel faced grave economic difficulties, and maintaining a strong conventional army became a great burden on the Jewish state.

These same concerns reinforced the need to be self-sufficient in nuclear power—that Israel could never trust any country to guarantee its security in the nuclear arena if it couldn't even count on them for conventional weapons.

On December 21, Ben Gurion told the Knesset (the Israeli Parliament) that Israel was constructing a nuclear reactor in the Negev in order to contribute to the development of the region.

The purpose of the 24-megawatt reactor would be to train scientists for agriculture, medicine, industry and science and to allow Israel to design and develop its own nuclear reactor within 10 to 15 years. Ben Gurion also reiterated that Israel had no intention of producing nuclear weapons.

But the secret was public and struck the world like a thunderbolt. The United States demanded assurances that Israel would produce no weapons, wanted explanations for the intent of the reactor and usage of the plutonium to be produced. In addition, the United States demanded inspection rights.

Ben Gurion was offended at the tone and insistence of the U.S. government. He told them his arrangement with the French was a delicate arrangement and was similar to the one between the Canadians and Indians. In addition, any plutonium produced by the reactor would be returned to the country supplying the enriched uranium.

He rejected the idea of foreign inspection—especially with the world press spotlighting every move Israel made involving nuclear technology.

The public disclosure and American pressure started an internal debate among Israel's leadership over nuclear independence. Should Israel spend the vast sums of money required to make nuclear weapons or rely on a powerful conventional army and air force? Although there were ups and downs to the debate, scientific development continued.

The entire government worked on the project. The Mossad, the intelligence service, and the Shin Beth, the Israeli secret service, contributed with shadowy achievements including the alleged theft of uranium from a nuclear facility in Pennsylvania in 1965 and possibly the hijacking of a vessel containing 200 tons of uranium.

The U.S. government, after a painstaking investigation, first determined 206 pounds of nuclear material vanished without a trace from the Nuclear Materials and Equipment Corporation, a small processing plant in Apollo, Pennsylvania, about 30 miles northeast of Pittsburgh.

This discovery started a massive investigation that involved the FBI, the Nuclear Regulatory Commission and the Department of Commerce. Altogether, government records showed 752 pounds of highly enriched uranium, enough to make almost 38 Hiroshima-sized atomic bombs, were lost during the plant's 20 years of operation. It remains unaccounted for today.

The manager of the plant at the time, a Jewish scientist who had close ties with Israel, was accused of diverting the uranium to Israel. He denied any involvement in the loss of the materials and government investigations failed to turn up any evidence as to where the missing materials went.

Security and protection of Dimona is tight and absolute. In 1967, during the Six-Day War, an Israeli French-built Ouragan fighter from the IAF was flying over the Negev. It was returning from a combat sortie over Jordan and was probably damaged. The plane angled toward Dimona about 25,000 feet overhead. Ground controllers warned the pilot to change his course; he was approaching prohibited air space. He continued on and failed to acknowledge the radio warning.

In a second, and now urgent, radio call he was ordered to make a turn away from Israel's nuclear facility.

No response. No course change.

Some speculated he had radio problems and was confused with his navigation. Others felt his oxygen system had failed at such altitude and he was unconscious.

Whatever the answer, it cost him his life.

After the second warning, the Israeli air defense forces using American-made Hawk missiles fired the deadly ground-to-air missiles at the plane which was blasted from the sky.

Israel is serious about the security of Dimona. It takes no chances when its national defense is involved.

And from that point on, every Israeli pilot developed respect for his own country's air defenses and has exercised special caution when in that particular area of the Negev.

As the years went by, bits and pieces of information came to light that Israel was developing or had the bomb.

The CIA concluded, and word slipped out, that Israel had nuclear weapons. U.S. intelligence concluded that Israel had manufactured all the necessary parts of nuclear bombs and could assemble them on short notice.

The sophistication of the Israeli nuclear program has been spelled out by Shai Feldman, a writer for the International Institute of Strategic Studies in London and research associate at the Center for Strategic Studies at Tel Aviv University.

He says the reactor at Dimona can produce enough plutonium for one bomb a year and that Israel has uranium enrichment capability.

"Such assessments have led observers to believe that by the late 1970s Israel had constructed some 10 to 20 nuclear weapons.

"But Israel has never confirmed any of this," Feldman concludes. "However, in the eyes of her neighbors, Israel is clearly regarded as being on the threshold of the nuclear era—if not across it."

In response to questions of its atomic capability, Israel's policy has always been to say, "We will not be the first to introduce nuclear weapons into the Middle East."

They have the weapon components—they just need to be assembled.

In 1974, the president of Israel, Ephraim Katzir, was giving a talk to a group of science writers. He gave them the big headline they were seeking when he said, "Israel has the potential to produce atomic bombs. If we need it, we will use it."

The Republic of South Africa is one of the world's largest sources for uranium. For different reasons, both countries are outcasts in the world of non-communist countries. For South Africa, because of apartheid, and for Israel, because it started its existence in conflict with the Arabs.

This status has given the two countries some common ground. They are suspected of having formed a top-secret alliance for the development of nuclear weapons to ensure their ultimate security in case of worldwide boycotts of arms.

Israel has allegedly provided much of the technical expertise over the years. The South Africans have provided much of the supplies, like uranium and delivery systems, although now South Africa is gaining rapidly in the technical area as well.

In addition to that, there is suspicion that both countries are working on a powerful neutron bomb—the kind of nuclear weapon that destroys people but not property.

Used in a tactical way in the Middle East, such a bomb would allow geographic control over the land mass, including the vital oil fields, yet not destroy the world's economy by leaving a radiation mess in the molten ruins of the oil-producing facilities in the event of war.

War could be fought with the powerful weapons and it wouldn't take a generation to clean up the radioactive debris. Such weapons have been rejected by the United States primarily because of liberal protests that such weapons might make nuclear war more acceptable.

There is no question in anyone's mind that Israel has nuclear capability. But there are several questions: Are the weapons assembled, ready to mount on aircraft or atop missiles, or do the parts for the bombs sit stored on a shelf somewhere and need to be assembled prior to being attached to a delivery system? How sophisticated and what small-size weapons has it achieved? And how many nuclear weapons has it managed to build and stockpile so far?

Some intelligence sources' estimates say they have about 60 bombs, including about 40 tactical weapons and about a half dozen megaweapons.

They are in preassembled units in "safe-deposit" boxes that require three keys—one each from representatives of the prime minister, minister of defense and state security. Those units would need to be put together to have an actual bomb. Estimates say that would take 48 to 72 hours.

Once Israeli scientists and officials got over the euphoria of developing the bomb, the realities of storing and maintaining the weapons set in. Nuclear weapons are complex to handle. Once assembled for use, they must be handled as delicately as a large egg. They must be protected from shock, immersion in water, dents or anything that could cause internal damage. They are hermetically sealed to avoid any radiation spills. No failures can be afforded.

When stored on the shelf, they must be designed to withstand corrosion and rust for decades.

U.S. weapons are clean and free of radiation leakage.

By contrast, the Soviet Union weapons are dirty and expose handlers to radiation—which also makes such weapons easy to detect and track while stored or in transit. Once a civilized nation possesses nuclear weapons, a strategy for usage must be developed.

The idea of a balance of retaliatory terror is the theory that supposedly keeps the Soviet Union from striking the United States—that is, the United States' ability to destroy the Russians even after and during the initial attack.

The common sense of that argument, some say, lacks credibility in the Middle East.

The Arab hatred for Israel is so strong that if any country there could develop powerful nuclear weapons and deliver them in such a way that the destruction of Israel could be guaranteed, they would do so regardless of the consequences.

But no Arab country has a bomb.

Even when an Arab state gets the bomb, there are going to be some basic questions: Who keeps the keys to the bunker where the bomb is stored? How does the bomb fit into Islam? Their religious goal is to regain the Holy Land—which means Jerusalem. If they destroy it, they can't reclaim it. There is a contradiction here. And despite popular belief, without Jews to dominate, the Arab reclamation of Israel is not complete.

Meanwhile, though, the Israelis have plenty of techniques for delivering their nuclear weapons—American-made Lance surface-to-surface missiles with a range of about 75 miles, plus two versions of the French Jericho surface-to-surface missiles. And, of course, the usual assortment of aircraft in the IAF including the F-16, F-15, F-4 Phantom, and the Israeli-built KFIR fighter bomber.

With all these delivery systems, plus the cruise missile, a nuclear gun, and the new Israeli-built LAVI fighter to be operational by 1990, Israel may be ready to go public with its nuclear capability and to develop a strategy designed to try for a balance of power in the Middle East. If that philosophy works, what Ben Gurion started may be one of the best undertakings and investments to ensure survival of the Jewish homeland.

The suspicion of Israel's development of nuclear weapons did not go unnoticed by their Arab enemies.

When the Middle East Six-Day War of 1967, the War of Attrition in the early 1970s, and the Yom Kippur War of 1973 failed to dislodge Israel, the Arabs recognized— although privately—that the Jews were in the Middle East to stay. The seriousness of such an event sank in. That's when the Arab countries decided they needed to take action of their own.

The hunger for Arab nuclear equality with Israel is an appetite that can be satisfied with no substitute.

On several occasions Israel has even suggested the idea of creating a nuclear-free zone in the Middle East.

Just as there is no trust of the Arabs by Israel, there is no trust of Israel by the Arabs.

Besides, the Arabs have had their teeth kicked in with every conventional war confrontation. There is strong sentiment that maybe super weapons, if possessed by the Arabs, would somehow change the balance of power. So the race is on.

All the Arab countries had three choices on how to acquire atomic weapons: (1) Acquire them from members of the nuclear club either as gifts or outright purchases. This is commonly known as the supermarket approach. (2) Develop facilities and technologies within their own country and build their own bomb. (3) Assist another country in nuclear development with an understanding of receiving a piece of the action, i.e., some bombs in return for the help. All these techniques have been and are being used by the Middle East countries.

But the intense nationalism and Arab rivalries have made it an "every man for himself" event.

Egypt was first to make serious efforts to possess nuclear capability. In the late fifties, Egyptian President Gamal Abdel Nasser set up several projects to boost Egypt's offensive capabilities which included development of an advanced jet fighter and engine for the fighter.

The fighter project was spearheaded by Willy Messerschmitt, the famous German engineer whose World War II ME 109 fighter helped Hitler nearly dominate Europe by controlling the skies. He was an outstanding airplane designer.

But Nasser's key project was to build surface-to-surface missiles with a range in the vicinity of 350 miles. At that time, possession of such delivery systems would give Egypt an offensive leg up over Israel. Nasser even boasted in one of his speeches that he could hit every target south of Beirut.

The secret missile project was known as 333 or Thalathat to Arabs. Before he learned of the Israeli nuclear efforts, Nasser planned to use the missiles to carry conventional explosive warheads. After revelation of the Dimona project, Nasser started two other warhead efforts: Ivis I and Operation Cleopatra. The former was the most uncontrolled and deadliest method of destroying people. It was simply to take radioactive isotopes, known as Cobalt 60, load them in the warhead atop the missiles of Project 333, and fire them off against Israel to pollute large areas of Nasser's enemy territory by spreading deadly radiation.

Several other versions of the project were to include poison gas, and chemical or biological materials in the warheads. The missiles could never be made accurate enough to be used or even test-fired with an explosive warhead aboard.

Operation Cleopatra was established to place nuclear warheads in the missiles. Egypt had no nuclear reactors at the time. The basis of this project was to use special techniques of centrifuge designed by the Dutch and West Germans to enrich low-grade uranium available on the open market. The project never really achieved its goals, even after huge investments of time and money. But word of it reached the Israeli Mossad who questioned whether the Egyptians had the expertise to make the project work, but they didn't take any chances.

While Ben Gurion was putting pressure on the West German government in 1962 not to cooperate with the Egyptians, letter bombs started exploding in the hands of key engineers on the Egyptian project. The casualties caused an epidemic of fear among leaders of the project and the workers.

Then Dr. Krug, a leading organizer in the jet engine program, mysteriously disappeared—never to be heard from again. Mossad's message was getting through. Work slowed and some engineers found other projects in which to get involved.

Two other efforts were made by Nasser to intimidate Israel. First, he tried to convince Leonid Brezhnev and the Soviet hierarchy to provide him with nuclear weapons. He made the same pitch to Mao Tse-tung. Both refused to trust him with the weapons. The Kremlin has zealously guarded its stockpile of nuclear weapons and any technology that could increase the spread of such power. Actually, Russia has been better about halting the spread of nuclear technology than the West.

But Nasser didn't totally fail with the Soviets. He got some kind of nuclear guarantee. Some believe those guarantees were what led him to start the 1967 Six-Day War—his primary objective being to destroy Israel's nuclear facilities in the Negev. The deal was that the Soviets would ship Russian-controlled nuclear weapons as a back-up to Egypt during such a war.

The Russian involvement was confirmed by the United States when a Soviet flag cargo ship clandestinely left the Black Sea port of Odessa and passed through the Dardanelles Strait where secret and sensitive U.S. monitoring equipment detected that the ship was loaded with nuclear weapons.

The freighter was tracked by the United States to the Egyptian port of Alexandria where it arrived October 15, 1967. Many believe this was the Soviet effort to neutralize any Israeli nuclear retaliatory threat that might have existed during that war.

Faced with the failure of the Six-Day War, the failure of his missile project, the failure of his jet engine program and his inability to possess nuclear weapons, Nasser was deeply concerned over Israeli power and their threat of nuclear domination over Egypt. Nasser developed a fear for the survival of Egypt.

His successor, Anwar Sadat, also realized the implication of Egypt's inferior power position. He also recognized the economic fact of Egypt's geography. Egypt is a desert—except for the 800-mile Nile River Valley which wanders north from Sudan to the Mediterranean Sea. It is along the Nile River banks where all major cities and population centers of Egypt are located.

The Nile is the lifeblood of Egypt and if polluted by Israeli nuclear radiation, nearly 4,000 years of Egyptian history would be finished.

Sadat realized—for the self-interest of his country— peace would now have to be made with Israel. The outgrowth of that realization, and the fact that Egypt could not neutralize the Israeli nuclear threat, was that peace with Israel was essential. Egypt would have to acknowledge that Israel was here to stay—an anathema to all Arabs, especially the PLO.

The outgrowth of this philosophy by Sadat was his extraordinary peace-making trip to Jerusalem in November 1977.

And with the stroke of a pen, Egypt was out of the expensive nuclear arms development program. What precious wealth Egypt had could be spent on her people.

But Sadat's Arab brothers were still charging full steam ahead. Syria does not have the wealth or talent to pursue construction of nuclear weapons. The Syrians are tough to deal with and the closest thing to a Soviet client state in the Middle East. The Russians have generously resupplied the Syrians with their best arms after each war and defeat by the Israelis.

But the Soviets will not provide them with nuclear weapons. Syria had negotiated an agreement with the Belgians and Swiss in 1981 to build what appears to be six nuclear power plants with a total output of 600 megawatts.

Like everyone, they emphasize that such a project would be strictly for peaceful purposes.

President Hafez Assad tried to get the French to sell him the technology to develop nuclear weapons but they refused. So the Syrians are out of the nuclear game at the present time.

Saudi Arabia really hasn't been interested in disturbing the balance of power in the Middle East. Most of their arms purchases have been defensive in nature. Their real concern hasn't been Israel, but some of their Arab brothers, especially Iraq and the Persians of Iran. But with the thrust of nuclear interest in the Middle East, the Saudis now are showing interest in nuclear power plants. All indications point to such interest being military in nature, since the country virtually floats on oil and has all the energy it will ever need.

There were reports in 1979 that the Saudis made a deal with the French as early as 1975 to acquire a nuclear reactor which would indicate they are going after a nuclear capability—but their efforts aren't on the fast track, yet.

The real race for nuclear power in the Arab world was to be between Libya and Iraq. Both countries have leaders that are totally Machiavellian. They subscribe to 16th century Niccolò Machiavelli's tome, *The Prince,* which says, "It is better to be feared than loved."

Both countries sit on land masses afloat with oil and have an intense hatred for Israel. Both countries have contempt for civilized law and order, and have been ruthless with their own people.

The leaders of both countries will stop at nothing to solidify their own power including political killings of anyone who opposes their regime. Neither has spent the vast sums available to them through oil sales to better their country or the lives of their citizens.

Both Gadhafi and Hussein are in the race to have the first Arab nuclear bomb, and both realize they can terrorize the world once they possess such power.

Each man realizes the power position in the Arab world goes to the winner of this particular specialized arms race. Gadhafi is funding development of a nuclear bomb by Pakistan—off his native soil. Hussein was trying to build his bomb right in Baghdad. And it was looking a lot like Hussein was going to win the race.

Meanwhile, his competition for the prize possession of nuclear weapons was pumping over a billion dollars into the Pakistani Project 706—The Muslim Bomb.

With that kind of financial stake, Gadhafi believed he had assured himself a share of the production of bombs —which would be a threat to Israel and for other terrorist activities worldwide.

Gadhafi has purchased an estimated $20 billion of Soviet-made military equipment—an enormous build-up for a desert nation of 3 million. Libya's 2,400 Soviet tanks and 500 warplanes constitute a force larger than France's tank divisions and Britain's Royal Air Force, according to some U.S. officials.

Some feel the build-up is part of a Soviet stockpile for future adventures, because the Libyans don't have enough personnel to properly operate all the war equipment in their possession.

In a speech in 1983 marking the anniversary of the closing of U.S. Wheelus Air Base in Tripoli, Gadhafi boasted that "we are now in a position to export terrorism, liquidation and arson to the heart of America."

He has made numerous efforts to help PLO terrorism

and threats against the West since that time. He has been associated with evidence linking Libya with subversion and terrorism in 45 countries since 1969, according to U.S. officials.

Gadhafi's first efforts to acquire nuclear weapons were his naive thoughts of approaching Chou En-lai of Red China and getting him to sell Libya nuclear devices. The Chinese leader, amazed at the suggestion, made it clear to the North African extremist that such items weren't sold "over the counter."

Frustrated by his failure, Gadhafi next turned to the Soviet Union to buy a nuclear reactor so he could build his own bomb. They have sold him a little 10-megawatt research reactor which is located in Siobu Bay along the Libyan coast. But the Russians have drawn the line on proliferation.

Since 1977, Libya and the Soviets have negotiated on building a 440-megawatt nuclear power plant—but as yet not one stone has been laid to begin construction. The Russians haven't even allowed him access to the technical knowledge to build a bomb.

The Soviets will use Gadhafi in ways that create problems for the United States and Israel, but plainly they don't want some wildman with that awesome power.

The Third World countries mistake communist intentions. The Soviets don't mind using the Arabs to stir up ferment in the Middle East by supplying conventional arms. But they never lose sight of their long-term objectives. The Arabs fit in with those objectives by causing unrest, discontent and efforts to destabilize legitimate governments. This eventually allows the Soviets to step in and bring peace to troubled countries, albeit peace without any personal freedoms in a totalitarian society. It also allows the Soviets to deny benefits of these countries' resources to the West.

The Arabs' limited objective of destroying Israel fits in with the overall objectives of the Soviets. So in reality, the Arabs are only tools of the Soviets who use them to cause turmoil throughout the Middle East—to further the Soviet ultimate goal of world domination.

Stymied, but with money because of Libya's vast oil reserves, Gadhafi went to Pakistan where most estimates say he has sunk over $1 billion into the Pakistani nuclear effort. Gadhafi made his top-secret deal with Pakistan in 1974 with then-Pakistan Premier Zulficar Ali Bhutto.

After some analytical thought, Gadhafi came up with the idea that the Israelis would never let an Arab country build a bomb on their own soil. How prophetic his insight turned out to be.

But he hasn't deviated from his goal to get nuclear weapons. He is stockpiling as much uranium as he can get from Niger in an effort to be Pakistan's sole source of the needed ingredient for nuclear weapons.

He bolstered that quest for uranium in 1985 by his efforts to take over Chad, which is directly to the south of Libya. A destitute country with hundreds of thousands of starving people, Chad's only asset is rich uranium. Gadhafi intends to own that supply as well.

The French oversaw both Niger and Chad as client states. They tolerated a major contribution to the Pakistani nuclear program by allowing Niger to sell 150 tons of uranium ore to Pakistan and 300 tons to Libya. Libya has no use for the unprocessed uranium—except to help Pakistan build the bomb. The ore was mined for Niger by a company under the control of the French Atomic Energy Commission.

The efforts by Pakistan to finish its bomb continue today. Gadhafi's support continues, although his part in that effort is as a bit player, albeit a large bit player.

Pakistan's real motive to build the bomb is to match archenemy India's nuclear effort that culminated in a "peaceful nuclear explosion" in 1974. No one has defined what a "peaceful nuclear explosion" is supposed to be. But it's believed that India either has built or is capable of building a small arsenal within months.

India and Pakistan have been at war three times since 1948. So there's real motivation for the continued efforts by Pakistan to complete its own bomb. And Gadhafi's acquisition of the bomb for his purpose is just a side effect of that effort.

Meanwhile, Hussein's efforts for Iraq to break into the nuclear club by building the bomb on his own territory were progressing nicely.

The stage was set; the race was on to build the first Arab bomb. And through skillful negotiations and using the clout of oil, Hussein was determined to build his own and be the first.

6

The French Connection

IN JULY 1960, Russia and Iraq made a deal for the Soviets to build a nuclear research reactor outside Baghdad. The project was started in 1963 and became operational in 1968. It started out as a two-megawatt facility and operated for ten years on one fueling.

In addition, the Soviet Union undertook the responsibility of training about 100 Iraqis in nuclear physics.

In 1978, the reactor needed refueling and the Iraqis got the Soviets to use more powerful fuel by upgrading from the low-level 10 percent enriched uranium to 80 percent enriched uranium. They also boosted power output to five megawatts.

But the 80 percent enriched uranium still was not enough to help Iraq get weapon-grade material. The greater the enrichment, the smaller the bomb and the easier it is to make—and the Soviets knew it took at least 90 percent enrichment to easily construct a bomb. Besides, the Soviets watched every move the Iraqis made with the use of their facility and a second small research facility they had built for Iraq. If they were to produce a bomb, the Iraqis came to the conclusion they needed independence from any oversight. The Iraqis, therefore, turned to western countries.

The oil embargo of 1973–74 gave the Arab countries a running start in acquiring something they had neither the money to buy nor talent to exploit.

When gasoline lines started to form in the United States and throughout Western Europe because of the Organization of Petroleum Exporting Countries (OPEC) embargo, the free world was awakened to just how fragile their lifestyles were.

It became apparent how dependent the industrialized world was on gasoline. One bottle of soda pop sold for what it cost to buy a half-dozen bottles of energy of the same size—gas was that taken for granted.

But that was all to change.

With the exception of water, no other liquid had such a sudden impact on modern society as did oil. The Arab world had a virtual stranglehold on the industrial world. An immediate and immense transfer of wealth occurred—in excess of a trillion dollars. But even more important, Arab countries began to receive the clout, attention and respect they had desired for so long.

Instead of being referred to as "camel drivers" and "sand niggers" who were welcomed nowhere in modern society, world leaders now not only received the wealthy Arab sheiks, but made pilgrimages to their countries to curry favor to ensure uninterrupted supplies of precious oil. There was great fear of crumbling economies of the West, and the efforts to build strong ties with oil-supplying Arab countries intensified.

One key side benefit was the opportunity for ambitious oil-producing countries to finally get a chance to crack the barrier to possession of nuclear weapons.

Iraq picked those countries most knowledgeable in nuclear technology, yet most vulnerable to Iraqi persuasion as their leading oil supplier. (With the fall of the Shah and near-anarchical situation in Iran, Iraq became the second-largest oil exporter in the world.)

The Iraqis approached the Japanese to build a larger nuclear facility than the Russians had. The Japanese government vetoed any nuclear cooperation. France was next.

In a nutshell, France was desperate to ensure continued supplies of oil. Iraq was France's second-largest supplier of oil providing more than 20 percent of its imported crude or $3 billion a year. Five years later, in December 1980 with the start of the Iran-Iraq war, that percentage was to fall to 3.6 percent.

Iraq's Hussein wanted nuclear weapons from the technology the French could supply, and was willing to spend oil revenues and make long-term military purchase commitments to get it.

In November 1975, Saddam Hussein made a nuclear shopping trip to Paris and struck a deal with French Prime Minister Jacques Chirac of the Giscard administration.

The deal did not enjoy unanimous endorsement in France. Andre Giraud, head of the French Nuclear Energy Committee, protested that the sale of nuclear equipment to Iraq might allow the Iraqis to join the Nuclear Club.

Other officials also protested.

But Chirac felt that immediate oil for France was vital and he ordered Giraud to keep his mouth shut or get fired. The French knuckled under to Iraqi demands.

The deal simply provided that France would build Iraq a 70-megawatt reactor, sell them six charges of 26 pounds of uranium each enriched to 93 percent, and help them establish a nuclear research and training center.

The Osiris reactor was to be built at Al-Tuwaitha, about 12 miles southeast of Baghdad near the shores of the Tigris River. It would cost $260 million and was scheduled for completion in 1981.

Iraq's part of the deal was to guarantee to sell France 70 million barrels of oil annually and to purchase French armaments—including jet warplanes, tanks, helicopters and missiles to the tune of $1.5 billion.

Other arms purchases included an integrated air defense system that would use Mirage fighters, mobile anti-aircraft missiles, radar installations and an electronic early-warning system said to be worth $600 million.

A total of 100 high-performance Mirage F-1 supersonic fighters were eventually sold by the French to Iraq at a cost of $800 million.

It was represented that Iraq was simply interested in nuclear power development and the nuclear equipment was solely for peaceful purposes, plus the agreement provided for international inspection—of course, at the times of Iraq's choosing—because Iraq was to sign the Nuclear Nonproliferation Treaty.

However, in September 1975, it's reported, a Lebanese newspaper article quoted Hussein as saying that the nuclear program was "the first Arab attempt toward nuclear arming, although the official declared purpose of construction of the reactor is not nuclear weapons."

A similar statement was made in 1977 by Naim Haddad, a member of Iraq's ruling Revolutionary Command Council. Said Haddad, "The Arabs must get a bomb."

In the face of such statements, the Israelis were not reassured by the fact that Iraq had signed the Nuclear Nonproliferation Treaty.

The Iraqi reactor was based on the type of reactors France already had in operation outside Paris, considered among the most advanced in the world.

The French government also agreed to train 600 Iraqi technicians and scientists for the first Arab "nuclear university," which could have become the nursery for nuclear physicists from all over the Arab world, including Israel's most bitter enemy—the Palestinians.

Even at that time, questions were raised in France about what real need oil-rich Iraq had for an advanced nuclear program. Experts said that the number of trainees vastly exceeded any conceivable need Iraq might have for scientists to manage a program to generate atomic power for strictly peaceful purposes.

Or as columnist Jack Anderson succinctly put it: "Iraq is a perfect example of what's wrong with the treaty [Nuclear Nonproliferation Treaty].

"On the face of it, the idea that a country wallowing in

oil would spend hundreds of millions of dollars to develop nuclear energy is absurd.

"The Iraqis, of course, haven't said that their reactors were supposed to produce electricity; they were to be merely 'research facilities.'

"But if they weren't to be power plants—which Iraq doesn't need—and they weren't for weapons production, what on earth were the reactors intended to be? Toys?

"Yet, despite this absurdity, Iraq is a member in good standing of the nonproliferation community.

"Israel, on the other hand, never signed the Nonproliferation Treaty. To the defenders of the treaty, this circumstance tends to make the Israelis the bad guys and the Iraqis the innocent victims," wrote Anderson.

"This, of course, is nonsense . . . There is no way Iraq can play a convincing role of well-meaning innocence.

"The Nonproliferation Treaty never raised the question of why a country with no nuclear reactors needed to stockpile uranium. The reason is, that it was officially none of their business. The treaty sets no limits on the amount of uranium a signatory nation can buy."

There were several official justification answers from France on the reason for the sale:

1. It received the money earned from the sale of the equipment.

2. Guaranteed stable supply of oil.

3. And Iraq had signed the Nuclear Nonproliferation Treaty and had agreed to the safeguards and inspections.

However, there was one problem that waved red flags on Iraq's intent. Iraq insisted on weapon grade 93 percent enriched uranium to power its reactor. The French lamely tried to sell them "caramel" fuel that was 6 to 8 percent enriched with a chemical bonding process that makes it impossible to extract plutonium from the spent fuel. After vigorous protests by the Iraqis, the French caved in. So the French sold Iraq the fuel necessary to make atomic bombs.

There are arguments that the spent fuel from the Iraqi plant was to be returned to France to ensure continued shipment of fresh fuel. If the French could be black-mailed into selling the equipment and highly enriched uranium in the first place, wouldn't the blackmail tactics continue to ensure an uninterrupted supply of reactor fuel?

Experts say the uranium to be furnished by the French could produce three to four nuclear weapons the size of the Hiroshima bomb. And by some estimates, they would have needed less than six months to turn the fuel into nuclear weapons.

Israeli intelligence kept track of the sale and fabrication of the equipment being sold to Iraq. Through diplomacy, Israel tried to ward off the danger, but it got nowhere. No one questioned whether Iraq's political character was suitable enough to be custodian of the nuclear weapons it was going to build. All recognized that Iraqi oil blackmail was involved.

France was to be the primary source of nuclear technology. For France, the relationship meant somewhere between $1 billion and $5 billion, depending upon who was doing the figuring.

But for the actual production of plutonium, the key ingredient of nuclear bombs, Iraq turned to oil-thirsty Italy. The Italians obtained one-fifth of their oil supply from Iraq. They weren't anxious to lose the oil and quickly made a $50 million agreement with Iraq to supply technical training for Iraqis and, most important-ly, provide a "hot cell," which is a shielded laboratory specially designed for handling radioactive substances and extracting plutonium.

The hot cell is usually used with large civilian power programs. But Iraq didn't have any power-producing facilities. There was simply no need for Iraq to have a hot cell, especially one as large as they were getting from Italy. The Iraqi facility was large enough to produce enough plutonium to have nuclear weapons within a year.

The Italians argued that Iraq planned to create a large

nuclear power industry and the research done with the hot cell would help Iraqi engineers cope with future technical problems.

American experts said, however, that Iraqi technicians, working with the complicated remote control equipment in a hot cell, would also learn how to separate plutonium from spent nuclear fuel.

The Carter administration criticized the purchase of this equipment, which can be used to produce radioisotopes for medical use as well as to separate plutonium.

Iraq also pressed Italy to sell them a heavy-water reactor—the type that uses natural uranium as fuel and easily produces large amounts of plutonium.

To help cement the deal, the Iraqis bought four Italian naval frigates. They contained eight American-built General Electric gas turbine engines valued at $11.2 million, which created some controversy in the United States about whether the United States was going against legislation designed to counter terrorism. By law, there was supposed to be public notification of exports to a State Department-listed terrorist country, if exports exceeded $7 million. Though Iraq was one of the four listed countries, there was no such notification.

More controversy developed over the numbers of Iraqis being trained in Italy. Experts protested that there were so many trainees in Italy, Iraq could be independent of foreign help in producing nuclear weapons in a relatively short period of time.

Nothing was said about Iraq's primitive ability to compete commercially with more sophisticated countries in the worldwide market for such nuclear abilities and research, or how the money could be better spent on education, health, water and sewage projects to better the way of life of Iraqi citizens. No matter how much the Iraqis learned, they would never be competitive in the world nuclear market.

Other nations were also helpful.

West Germany was involved too.

But for public consumption the Germans protested their innocence.

All they did, was sell a huge nuclear package to Brazil. That way they skirted the Nuclear Nonproliferation Treaty of which West Germany was a signatory.

The deal with Brazil was for the construction of nine atomic power plants at a cost of $10 billion.

Then Brazil simply resold much of this to Iraq.

Iraq intended to buy four of the plants from Brazil.

This program made no sense.

This deal with Brazil was considered important.

As part of the package, Brazil was supposed to be receiving the technology of uranium enrichment from West Germany.

Standard electrical engineering says no one power plant should be more than 10 percent of the total power produced by a city or country.

With total electrical consumption of all Iraq being a little over 4,000 megawatts, each of the proposed power plants would provide 50 percent of the current electrical usage of the entire country—or all four would have doubled the electrical output of Iraq.

Plants that enrich uranium use enormous amounts of electricity. It has been estimated that in the mid-1970s, 15 percent of the electrical power generated in the United States was used in the enrichment of uranium.

The reason isn't clear. Some say it is the high price to construct the power reactors; but whatever the reason, no construction has begun on these facilities in Iraq.

With an estimated 192,000 tons of uranium reserves and a dependence on Iraq for 40 percent of its oil imports, the Brazilians signed the agreement that covered help with construction of nuclear power plants in Iraq, including provisions of nuclear technical expertise and the supplying of slightly enriched uranium.

The Iraqis assured the Brazilians 160,000 barrels of oil a day for 13 years as their part of the deal.

There was a powerful effort by the Iraqis to hoard all

the uranium they could get their hands on. Besides the highly enriched supply from France and this new batch from Brazil, Iraq bought 138 tons of "yellowcake" or uranium dioxide, from Portugal in 1980, after threatening to shut off their oil supply, and 100 tons from Niger.

In addition, West Germany sold Iraq 10 tons of natural and depleted uranium which can be irradiated into plutonium. They also intended to buy from Morocco in the future.

The Iraqi effort to buy and stockpile yellowcake raised eyebrows of those in the industry.

In addition, Iraq has had negotiations with Somalia which recently discovered large quantities of uranium.

There were also stories that Iraq and nuclear bomb possessor India signed a deal for uranium. They tried to buy uranium from other countries as well, using subterfuge, arms deals and other undercover operations— without success.

If there were a legitimate need and reason for nuclear power for Iraq, certainly all this subterfuge wouldn't have been necessary.

The reactor project alone wasn't an isolated project. The Iraqis were also investing huge sums in acquiring missiles technology and negotiating with a number of Western and Soviet countries for the manufacture of an 1,800-mile-range ground-to-ground missile system which could only be intended to deliver a nuclear warhead.

The toothless Nuclear Nonproliferation Treaty (NPT) was in essence used as a decoy to allow nations to make money and to sell nuclear technology with a clear conscience that it supposedly stopped the spread of bomb-making.

France justified to itself and the rest of the world the sale of nuclear information and equipment by the fact that Iraq had signed the NPT and agreed to all the safeguards and inspections of the Vienna-based agency.

The treaty was designed to stop the spread of nuclear

weapons, especially to radical or unstable regimes, or to fanatical, violent groups that would threaten to make the world even more unsafe.

It was pushed by the Big Five—full-fledged members of the nuclear club with large arsenals—the United States, the Soviet Union, Britain, France and China.

Since 1968, some 117 of the world's 170 nation states have signed the treaty. It prohibits signatories from building or selling nuclear weapons and provides for the international inspection of peaceful nuclear facilities.

A corollary organization is the International Atomic Energy Agency (IAEA). A United Nations organization, the IAEA has established so-called safeguards on the peaceful use of nuclear fuels and conducts on-site inspections to ensure that its safeguards are being properly implemented. It has no real enforcement powers.

In addition, it seeks to encourage use of civilian nuclear power, thereby spreading nuclear technology. The two purposes seem at conflict with each other.

There is a lot of political hiding behind the phrasing of "safeguarding" implied in the NPT and IAEA. There is no such thing as safeguarding by the IAEA. Their system basically consists of monitoring, information gathering and reporting. Nothing more. There are no agreed-upon penalties for violators.

The philosophy of the safeguard system is that diversion of nuclear material (not equipment) from peaceful to military use can be discouraged through the risk of being detected.

Then the thought is that the international community will take some unspecified appropriate action to prevent actual construction of weapons.

If the violator country refuses to do anything about world opinion, then the only unlikely option to halt such efforts probably would be war, and who is going to undertake that action?

The NPT is violated only when nuclear fuel or uranium is actually converted to weapons.

Inspections usually consist of two or three experts

scrutinizing shipment books and verifying that no seals or valves have been tampered with. Government officials can postpone or cancel inspection visits and sometimes do.

IAEA officials have admitted "we control and account for the fissile materials only. We don't look for secret tunnels or bunkers."

In essence, the inspectors are bookkeepers, not investigators. They send up no alarms when a government's nuclear program involves sophisticated technology or fuel stockpiles far in excess of what its nuclear power program seems to warrant.

So when a country like Iraq signs the treaty, it is perfectly free to press on in weapon development without fear of violating it. Then, when it is ready to build an actual bomb, the escape provision of the treaty can be invoked. That provision simply is, if a signatory to the NPT feels its security is threatened, it makes such a declaration and within 90 days can cancel out of the NPT.

Under the guise of being an NPT signatory, a country can simultaneously pursue a civilian nuclear program and a military program until it is time to construct the actual weapons and then withdraw from the treaty.

The only teeth in the NPT are that unspecified actions might come from aroused world opinion. In reality, joining NPT for a nation bent on developing nuclear weapons has great propaganda value—until the weapons exist—and then it isn't worth the paper it is written on.

If Iraq tore up the Shatt al-Arab Agreement and went on to invade neighboring Iran, why couldn't it just as easily have scratched out its signature on the NPT?

The only true way to prevent the spread of nuclear weapons is for countries with the technological know-how to stop the sale of nuclear equipment. That means West Germany, Italy, France, Belgium, Spain, Switzerland, Canada, Brazil, Argentina, Britain, Sweden, The Netherlands and the United States.

The chances of that happening are nonexistent. No

country wants to lose out on sales revenue that might go to a competitor. It's big dollars. So the nuclear arms race is on, with suppliers all pointing the guilty finger of nuclear proliferation at their competitors as the violators.

As the number of countries working with uranium and especially plutonium increases, so does the opportunity for terrorists to gain possession of these deadly materials.

Even in the United States where you would expect security to be very tight, tests by law enforcement officials have shown that it would be possible for terrorists to steal enough plutonium to make a bomb. And security arrangements in other countries may be less stringent.

Possessing plutonium does not in itself give terrorists a nuclear capability, but any group that made the effort to steal it would probably have developed or stolen the means to make it into a bomb.

The real threat to society is not the launching of bombs between the United States and the Soviet Union. There is too much precise and carefully controlled accounting for such an accident to happen. The real threat is a terrorist-oriented country or group gaining possession of a nuclear bomb. They are not responsible people and have nothing to lose in using it to further their goals.

Many Middle East terrorists operate with the philosophical belief that to die in action for one's cause brings hallowed afterdeath glory in heaven. So does it make a difference if a fanatical suicide mission is conducted with conventional explosives or nuclear ones? Those taking on the mission are just as dead by either explosion. And what a distinction to have been the first to trigger a nuclear device on your enemy!

Israeli intelligence set up a special unit to watch, gather and collect information on France's construction of Iraq's nuclear equipment. The threat was serious. If the politicians couldn't work out a solution, there were always other ways.

7

An Inspector's View

FOR MORE THAN three years Roger Richter was a nuclear safeguards inspector with IAEA. After resigning in June 1981 to make his concerns public, he was immediately invited to testify before the Senate Foreign Relations Committee on the Israeli raid at Tammuz. As an expert who was to check on a reactor's ability to convert uranium into bombs, he had some specific thoughts and experiences.

This chapter is adapted from his testimony and appeared in the *Washington Post* on June 23, 1981.

"SUPPOSE YOU WERE A REACTOR INSPECTOR"
by Roger Richter

Imagine that you are a nuclear safeguards inspector who will shortly be going to Iraq to conduct an inspection.

You have to imagine yourself as a national of the Soviet Union or another Eastern bloc country.

Since 1976, all inspections performed in Iraq have been conducted by Soviets or Hungarians. Countries have the right to veto inspectors from whatever countries they choose—a right which they regularly exercise.

As an accepted inspector, you must keep in mind that any adverse conclusions you might reach as a result of your inspections would have to take into account your country's sensitivity to how this information might affect relations with Iraq.

In preparing for the inspection, you must first give the government of Iraq several weeks' notice of your planned inspection and obtain a visa. The government may agree with the date or could, as has recently been the case, suggest you postpone or change your plans.

You are aware that since Iraq is a signatory of the Nuclear Nonproliferation Treaty, the only facilities subject to your examinations are those that Iraq has declared to the International Atomic Energy Agency, as containing either thorium, natural or depleted uranium in metal or oxide form, or plutonium.

Natural uranium in the form of U_3O_8, commonly known as yellowcake, is not subject to safeguards, despite its potential for easy conversion to target specimens for plutonium production.

You are not entitled even to look at the other facilities if Iraq has not adhered to its obligation under NPT to report to the IAEA that material subject to safeguards is located in these facilities. You are aware that the role of the inspector is limited to verifying only material declared by Iraq or France.

You have no authority to look for undeclared material.

Your job is to verify that the declared material accountancy balance is correct.

The IAEA does not look for clandestine operations. The IAEA, in effect, conducts an accounting operation.

The amount and level of enrichment of the reactor fuel elements is indicated on your computer printout. But you notice that 100 tons of uranium in the form of U_3O_8 is not on the list. This is not an oversight but a reflection of the fact that, even though Portugal reported the shipment to the IAEA, it is only a formality; the 200,000 pounds of U_3O_8 is not subject to safeguards.

Had this uranium been in a slightly reduced form, such as UO_3, it would have been under safeguards; but this loophole could enable Iraq to do as it pleases with the U_3O_8.

And so long as it does not report that the U_3O_8 has been converted into a material that is in the safeguarded category, you have no right to inquire of its whereabouts.

You are disturbed by this because you realize that in the other Italian-supplied fuel-processing equipment, which is not under safeguards, Iraq possesses the capability to convert, in a rather simple fashion, the U_3O_8 to UO_3 or, even better, to uranium metal.

As much as 17 to 24 kilograms of plutonium could be produced each year with the Osiris reactor.

Even if only one-third of this amount were produced in the first few years of operation of the reactor, through the use of the attendant processing facilities, Iraq could acquire a stockpile of plutonium sufficient to make several atomic bombs.

Equally disturbing to you as an inspector is the realization that under the present negotiated agreement between the IAEA and Iraq, you will be limited to only three inspections per year, usually spaced at approximately four-month intervals.

By the time you arrive to verify the declared inventory of fuel elements that power the reactor, all evidence of illicit irradiations could be covered up.

You may now be wondering what exactly an inspector actually does in the course of performing a safeguard inspection of the Osiris nuclear complex.

Your inspection assignment is actually quite narrowly focused.

First, you will sit down with the operator of the nuclear reactor and review your computer listing of the nuclear material that has been declared to the IAEA. You will determine that the amount recorded by the operator is consistent with the amount reported to the IAEA by France.

If there is new, unirradiated fuel in the inventory, you will determine that the elements have not been replaced by dummy replica fuel.

This is particularly important in the case of the Osiris fuel, since it would be a relatively easy matter to melt down the weapons-grade highly enriched uranium fuel plates for use in a nuclear bomb.

If the fuel elements are already in the reactor and have been irradiated, the inspection procedure normally requires that you visually identify the fuel elements. They can normally be observed under the approximately 20 feet of water.

To confirm that these elements are not dummies, you have the right to ask the operator to turn on the reactor. You should then see a characteristic blue glow.

You will now return to Vienna and report that your inspection disclosed no discrepancies between the operator's records and that of the agency.

The difficult part of the job is that you must prepare yourself mentally to ignore the many signs that may indicate the presence of clandestine activities going on in the facilities adjacent to the reactor—facilities that you were not permitted to inspect.

You will try to forget that you have just been party to a very misleading process.

I was prompted a year ago to write of my concerns about Osiris to the Department of State U.S. mission to the IAEA:

"The available information points to an aggressive, coordinated program by Iraq to develop a nuclear weapons capability during the next five years.

"As a nuclear safeguards inspector at the IAEA, my concern and complaint is that Iraq will be able to conduct this program under the auspices of the Nonproliferation Treaty and while violating the provisions of the NPT.

"The IAEA safeguards are totally incapable of detecting the production of plutonium in large-size material test reactors under the presently constituted safeguards arrangements.

"Perhaps the most disturbing implication of the Iraqi nuclear program is that the NPT agreement has had the effect of assisting Iraq in acquiring the nuclear technology and nuclear material for its program by absolving the cooperating nations of their moral responsibility by shifting it to the IAEA.

"These cooperating nations have thwarted concerted international criticism of their actions by pointing to Iraq's signing of NPT, while turning away from the numerous, obvious and compelling evidence which leads to the conclusion that Iraq is embarked on a nuclear weapons program."

8

The French Mysteries

THE ISRAELI GOVERNMENT exerted all the quiet subtle pressure it could on France to stop the sale of nuclear equipment and the delivery of highly enriched uranium to Iraq. The French turned a deaf ear.

Next, the Israelis pulled out all the stops to enlist American support to put the pressure on the French to stop the deal. This included using a variety of Jewish organizations in the United States as well as government-to-government contacts.

The United States had been successful in blocking the sale of nuclear technology to South Korea after Washington put intense pressure on Seoul, and then on the French, to let the South Koreans cancel the purchase of nuclear equipment.

More pressure finally delayed and eventually canceled nuclear technology transfers to Pakistan, although deliveries of many blueprints and some equipment had already been made.

Israeli intelligence watched in 1976 as Iraq's Atomic Energy Commission annual budget leaped from $5 million to $70 million.

But all the pressure tactics had no effect on the French sale to Iraq.

As construction proceeded, Israeli officials debated how best to stop the reactor from going into operation, and how to send a message to France, Iraq and the rest of the world that this project must not be completed.

There were discussions about sabotage of the equipment before it left France and intimidation of people working on the project. Would the dirty tricks campaign used on the Germans working for Egypt's Nasser missile project work again?

One Israeli official is reported to have said: "Nasser's missile experts were Germans, mostly former Nazis. These people were Frenchmen and Italians. We couldn't repeat old tactics."

Work on the Iraqi reactor cores by the French company contracted for the job was finished in early April 1979. The equipment was crated up in an airplane hangar-type building in the port of La Seyne-sur-Mer near Toulon on the French Mediterranean coast. Within days, it was to be shipped to Iraq.

Besides the cores, the cargo consisted of a metal block designed to house atomic batteries for one of the reactors and other components for the reactors.

About this same time (March 28, 1979), the nuclear accident at Three Mile Island outside Harrisburg, Pennsylvania, produced strong vocal protests against nuclear power. Hundreds of leftist demonstrators rallied outside the Industry Ministry in Paris in angry protest. The protests were being staged in France to criticize President Valéry Giscard d'Estaing's nuclear development programs. He had vowed not to slow down France's nuclear energy program which is considered vital to the economic stability of virtually oilless France.

France had 15 nuclear energy plants in operation and another 27 under construction.

Alongside the Iraqi equipment were apparatus designed to load nuclear fuel into a reactor for a Belgian firm and a West German-ordered lid for a container to store radioactive materials at a nuclear plant at Kalkar in the Rhineland Palatinate.

Security around the building owned by the Nuclear

Division of the private Mediterranean naval and industrial firm was poor; it consisted of three guards who were not properly patrolling the premises.

Sometime after midnight on April 6, 1979, a team of as many as seven skillful saboteurs slipped into the building undetected.

With precise and deliberate care that came from inside detailed knowledge of the secret programs, layout and security arrangements of the plant, the intruders placed three separate charges of plastic explosives.

At 3:00 A.M. on that Friday, a deafening thunderous roar blasted through the town followed by two additional explosions. The windows and much of the roof blew out of the hangar-like building. Somehow the three night watchmen escaped injury. But the Iraqi, Belgian and German equipment lay in a pile of rubble.

The demolished equipment was valued at $11 million and in the three years of production, 300,000 man-hours had been spent constructing it.

The Iraqi dream had been delayed for a while.

Immediately, the French authorities started a secret investigation. They remained tight-lipped about their findings.

A group no one had ever heard of before or since, the "Group of French Ecologists," claimed responsibility for the bombing. An anonymous telephone caller told the French newspaper, Le Monde, the name of the group and that the equipment was bombed to "neutralize machines that threaten the future of human life."

He went on to say the reactor accident in Harrisburg, Pennsylvania, "demonstrated once again the dangers of nuclear energy. The Harrisburg catastrophe proved to us the dangers of the atomic industry. We have turned to action and we will do what is necessary to safeguard the French people and the human race from nuclear horrors," the caller concluded.

Police said the blasts were not the work of amateurs but clearly the efforts of well-organized professionals experienced and skilled in handling explosive devices.

There was a great deal of guessing in the French press as to who was responsible for the blasts.

Some of the more remote possibilities involved the CIA, Libya's Moammar Gadhafi, the PLO, Russians, and Syrians—each of whom had a justified reason.

But when all the dust settled, there were only two serious scenarios. The *International Herald Tribune* speculated the raid had been carried out by French secret service officials in the French government who came to feel the Iraqi deal might imperil other countries in the Middle East, and that would be against the best interests of France.

And, of course, there was the Mossad. The Israelis had the strongest motivation for carrying out the attack, but no evidence was ever found that clearly pointed the finger at the Israeli secret service or anyone else.

Following the sabotage at La Seyne-sur-Mer, French Prime Minister Raymond Barre, during his official visit to Baghdad in July 1979, tried to convince the Iraqis to accept a different core design for the Osiris that would use low-grade uranium rather than weapon-grade fuel.

This was a second effort to get the Iraqis to use the caramel fuel, but the Iraqis adamantly demanded a duplicate of the destroyed core and the initial loading of 26 pounds of enriched uranium.

President Hussein warned Barre that if he refused, he would risk an oil cutoff and the cancellation of French arms purchases.

On his return to Paris, Barre had a meeting with President Giscard d'Estaing and the outcome was that the French government agreed to deliver a replica of Osiris and the enriched fuel to Iraq without conditions.

Whether or not Israel's secret agents were involved, the French-Iraqi nuclear project was dogged by sabotage and mysterious deaths.

A year after the La Seyne-sur-Mer incident, the Egyptian-born head of the Iraqi program was found bludgeoned to death in his Paris hotel room.

In the summer of 1980, Yahia al-Meshad, 50, went to

France to check out some equipment and to verify that the uranium to be shipped was 93 percent.

After a week of visiting the French Nuclear Center and other facilities scattered around the countryside, he returned to his Paris hotel on Friday evening, June 13. On the way upstairs to his room, a French prostitute, Marie Claude Magal, 32, made a "friendly" proposal to al-Meshad. He rejected it, entered his room and closed the door. She said she stood outside, hoping he'd reconsider her offer. He didn't, but while there, she heard voices in the room.

The next morning, the housekeepers found al-Meshad's battered body, his head bashed in, lying on the carpet in a pool of drying blood. It was four days before the police allowed the newspapers to publish the story. The authorities first wanted to notify Iraq of his death.

On July 1, Marie Magal was interrogated by French police about what she saw and heard that fateful night. She was the key witness in the investigation. As the probe continued, French authorities sought out Marie for a second session of questioning—only to find she had been killed in a hit-and-run auto accident on July 12.

The Mossad was first on everyone's list as probably suspects for these deaths, although the Israelis vehemently denied that they were to blame.

French police came to the conclusion that al-Meshad's death was too sloppy a job for such a professional outfit as the Mossad. Some Egyptian sources claimed Syrian agents working for the Russians had committed the crimes. They claim the motive was to get someone in Meshad's room and make copies of his notes and diary to learn what was going on at this stage of Iraq's nuclear development. The prostitute was supposed to delay Meshad from entering his room.

Whoever was to blame, his death sent ripples of fear among other workers on the project. Then about a month later, hidden bombs wrecked the Rome offices of SNIA Techint, the Italian nuclear company working in Iraq.

The same day, there was an unsuccessful attempt to assassinate a French scientist working on the Osiris project.

In spite of all these activities, the Iraqi project remained on schedule for completion in 1981.

9

The Reactor

THE IRAQI NUCLEAR program was put in commission in 1968 along the Tigris River at Al Tuwaitha, about 12 miles southeast of Baghdad, with the installation of the Soviet two-megawatt thermal power reactor. It was placed in operation in 1968 and was refueled in 1978 with the power upped to five megawatts.

The Russians also supplied Iraq with a laboratory to produce radioisotopes, special physics labs and some other smaller facilities.

The Iraqis were now in the rudimentary stages of nuclear research. But it was to become more sophisticated.

After conclusion of the deal with the French, additional ground was staked out for the construction of Project Tammuz 17—the name given the overall project of French-installed equipment.

Within that project were Tammuz I and Tammuz II.

Tammuz I included the 70-megawatt French reactor originally known as Osiris and renamed by the Iraqis as Osirak. It was this reactor that could convert uranium into needed plutonium to build a nuclear bomb.

The Italian "hot cell," which could separate plutonium from uranium, was also located in this part of the overall complex and was known as Project 30 July.

Tammuz II was the one-megawatt nuclear reactor

obtained from the French for research. The name of the reactor was Isis before being renamed Tammuz II.

For Tammuz I, the Iraqis originally wanted a French reactor that was producing plutonium for the French military as well as producing civilian power.

Power generation would have been good diversion cover for snooping countries by having Iraq produce electrical power, and at the same time, rapid production of bomb material.

The reactor they desired was a 500-megawatt uranium graphite gas reactor that could produce electricity and nearly 100 pounds of plutonium a year for bombs. The French refused to sell this reactor. But after protracted talks, the French reached a compromise to sell the Iraqis one of the most advanced research reactors designed to study new fuel elements, the 70-megawatt Osiris.

This reactor had never been sold to a foreign power before. Previously, it had been restricted to use on French soil only.

Osiris was an Egyptian god of the dead. Since the Iraqis were angered by the Egyptians making peace with Israel, they modified the name to Osirak.

It was not an electric power-generating reactor. A power-generating reactor runs on barely-enriched uranium. Such a reactor was of no use to the Iraqis since it did not use enriched fuel.

For research reactors, the French have developed caramel fuel which is a taffy-like uranium fuel. It is cheaper and can do virtually the same research that highly enriched uranium can do—except produce bomb-grade plutonium. That was the fuel that was rejected by the Iraqis.

They insisted on highly enriched uranium. And they got it.

Two parts of the Osirak reactor were underground. One was a drive mechanism for the control rods in the reactor, which was virtually under the reactor itself and was accessible during operation. The other part was something new called the neutron guide chamber. It was about ten feet underground, and was off to the side of the reactor. The French say it is used in research on effects of neutron radiation.

This new chamber to the Osirak reactor was probably the reason Israeli intelligence surmised there was a secret chamber below ground where the uranium fuel or any plutonium produced by the uranium could be diverted to make an atom bomb.

After Operation Babylon, Begin referred to this as a secret chamber. The French denied there was anything secret about it and released the drawings to back up their claim.

From Italy, the Iraqis bought four research facilities which included a radio-chemistry laboratory equipped for reprocessing irradiated fuel elements—more commonly known as separating plutonium—which could be used for nuclear bombs.

Saddam Hussein also pushed Italy to sell him a heavy-water reactor using natural uranium as fuel. This reactor could have produced large amounts of plutonium extracted in a radio chemistry lab to make bombs.

In the fall of 1980, fearing Iranian air attacks against the facility because of the war with Iraq, France and Italy pulled out most of their 150 technicians. About 25 were left behind.

The Iranians didn't disappoint those watching the war. They attacked the plant September 30, 1980, causing relatively minor damage. The reactors themselves were not damaged, but some labs and service facilities were hit. Water cooling systems of the reactors were damaged by a direct hit and some plumbing installations and piping systems were destroyed.

The Iranian raid was a failure.

Iraq's grand dream of an overnight victory over Iran faded.

As the war between the two enemies stabilized into a long-term conflict, the French and Italian technicians returned to work in February 1981.

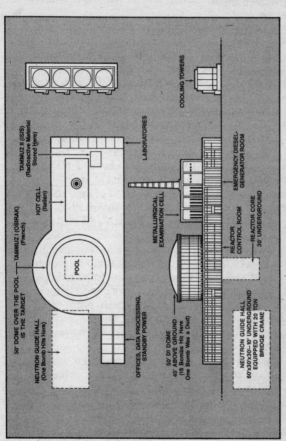

NEUTRON GUIDE HALL
(One Bomb Hits Here)

50' DOME OVER THE POOL — TAMMUZ I (OSIRAK) (French)
IS THE TARGET

POOL

HOT CELL
(Italian)

TAMMUZ II (ISIS)
(Radioactive Material
Stored Here)

LABORATORIES

10' DI DOME
40' ABOVE GROUND
(15 Bombs Hit Here
One Bomb Was a Dud)

OFFICES, DATA PROCESSING,
STANDBY POWER

METALLURGICAL
EXAMINATION CELL

COOLING TOWERS

NEUTRON GUIDE HALL
60'x30'x-10' UNDERGROUND
EQUIPPED WITH 20 TON
BRIDGE CRANE

REACTOR CONTROL ROOM

REACTOR CORE
30' UNDERGROUND

EMERGENCY DIESEL-
GENERATOR ROOM

The Osirak reactor building was similar to the French ones built in France. However, the neutron guide hall was new. This hall was mistaken by Begin as a secret chamber. All bombs hit the reactor dome except one that went into the neutron guide hall. Fourteen of the bombs that penetrated the dome exploded; one was a dud.

They lived with their families in a housing compound about 500 yards away from the reactors outside the immediate defensive perimeter—a horseshoe-shaped earthen revetment surrounding the facility on three sides.

The French had an unpublished agreement with Iraq that was to keep French scientists at the site until 1989. Even newly elected French President Mitterrand was unaware of this agreement until after the attack.

Access to the reactor area was tightly controlled and restrictive. There were at least two checkpoints that construction and plant workers proceeded through daily, one of which included airport-type X-ray machines. Iraqi guards in combat fatigues strolled around the work areas with Soviet automatic rifles slung over their shoulders. Closed-circuit TV monitors checked all activity. There was no privacy inside the reactor area.

Some of the workers were suspected of dual roles. Iraqi workers and security agents were disguised as workers trying to spot spies among the French and Italian workers.

It is believed some of the workers fed intelligence information to the Mossad. None of them knew who the others were and it was too dangerous to be snoopy.

The area was surrounded by both a concrete fence and a sophisticated electrical fence which pinpointed any clandestine efforts to enter the area. On the outside area, jeep-type vehicles with armed guards and two-way radios patrolled.

An earthen berm about 100 feet high was being constructed around the area. Though it wouldn't be completed until after the air raid, it would not have made a difference concerning the accuracy of the Israeli bombs.

The compound was heavily fortified against air attack. On the surrounding walls and in front of them were anti-aircraft armament (AAA) batteries and surface-to-air missile (SAM) sites, including the necessary radar facilities to lock in on any attacking aircraft. These defense armaments extended out from the complex to a radius of about two miles.

Roads leading to the reactor site from Baghdad had armed checkpoints.

All this security for what was billed as a simple nuclear research facility.

There were a variety of separate structures in the compound area which was roughly one-quarter mile square (see chart).

The first structure was the Soviet research area which included labs, biology studies, lecture rooms and administrative offices. Surrounded with hedges and flowers, it was about 250 feet square.

South of that was a fuel fabrication site purchased from the Italians. It was not a large facility and the Iraqis claim this was to be used to train personnel to back up a nuclear power plant program. Many believe this facility was vital in assembling uranium packages to help in the production of plutonium.

In the southeast corner of the facility was a large building with a huge machine shop complex.

In the southwest corner was a radioactive waste facility which was bought from France. It was for training personnel in encapsulation of radioactive waste in concrete, and working on other techniques for treating radioactive waste.

Slightly to the north between the machine shop and radiation waste facility were Tammuz I and II.

It was a long rectangular building with a white concrete dome or cupola about 40 feet above ground level in the center of the building. The dome was about 50 feet in diameter. At most, the dome was only a few inches thick. This dome was to become the target of the Israeli Air Force in the attack that would rock the world.

The Tammuz I reactor was under the dome. In essence, it was an open-top swimming pool full of light water sunk into the ground about 30 feet with a variety of tubes and plumbing crisscrossing through the pool of water.

All the plumbing of coolants, fuel rods, neutron beams —in other words, all the guts of the reactor—are submerged under water in this pool. Had this facility been built above ground, as most are, damage from the attack would have been even more extensive.

The dome covered the reactor to provide an airtight vacuum to ensure that any slight leakage of radioactive substances from the reactor would be sucked into the facility rather than drift out into the atmosphere.

There was a ground-level control room adjacent to the reactor. Next to the reactor room on the west side of the building were the hot cells purchased from the Italians. Beyond these was the small Tammuz II reactor. This smaller reactor was activated in February 1980.

It is believed it was in this area that the 26 pounds of enriched uranium was stored in underground water-filled storage tanks to keep it from having a chain reaction before being placed in the reactor.

The fuel had "gone critical" (or to the point at which a sustained reaction could be maintained) to test its efficiency just days before the attack. This verified to Israeli intelligence that the reactor would have been fueled and the place would have been radioactive had the air strike been delayed.

Reportedly, the French had pre-irradiated the first batch of uranium in order to poison it with radiation to make it too hot to divert it from power generation to nuclear weapons. At this time Iraq didn't have the necessary remote handling devices.

On the east side of the reactor building was the neutron guide hall which was about 60 feet long, 30 feet wide and 10 feet underground. The top was covered with several feet of concrete and the rest was dirt. The chamber itself was about 30 feet high. Sophisticated equipment was scheduled to be moved into this building the day after the attack.

A 20-ton bridge crane could travel on steel beams along the length of the room.

This was the facility Begin claimed was a secret

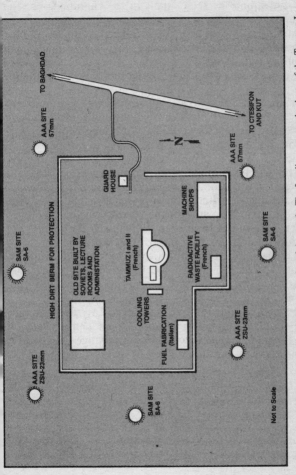

The nuclear reactor complex as it looked on the day of the attack. The Israeli target was the dome of the Tammuz I building in the center of the complex.

chamber for developing atomic bombs. The French said it was to be used in the plant's research on effects of neutron radiation. Technicians in the chamber were to target materials placed in the reactor at the bottom of the swimming pool with neutrons produced by the fissioning uranium fuel in the reactor.

On the northern side of the facility were the entrance hall, offices, data processing center and a standby power area.

Before and after the attack there have been opinionated arguments in the scientific community as to just how easily the reactor could have produced bomb-grade plutonium and how long it would take to do so.

Richard Wilson, professor in nuclear and high energy physics and head of the physics department of Harvard University, was provided an expense-paid trip by Iraq to visit the reactor site about a year and a half after the Israeli attack. He came to the conclusion that, as constructed, it would have been difficult for the reactor to produce plutonium. Not impossible, but difficult.

In the scientific community there were some questions about the reactor. In the political community, no one questioned the long-range intent of Iraq to use the technology to build themselves the bomb.

Few people question Iraq's ability to have done so, but many question how long it would have taken. Nevertheless, the mere fact this facility existed changed the course of Middle East politics.

10

The Debate

THE FIRST HINTS of knowledge to the Israeli leadership of the transfer of nuclear technology to Iraq created ripples of concern.

As time passed and the evidence mounted, Israeli leadership became convinced that the potential threat of nuclear weapons from Iraq aimed at Israel was real—and those ripples turned to a tidal wave of alarm.

Like all national survival issues, there were pros and cons to be debated concerning what actions to take.

With Israeli leadership before the raid, and world opinion thereafter, issues were raised. Were the Iraqis really simply interested in nuclear power and research as they publicly professed? Were they actually incapable of producing the bomb with their facilities? Could the Iraqis have been bluffing about building a bomb? With limited Israeli knowledge and ambiguity of the actual Iraqi capability, could the Israelis have been tricked and forced to accede to Iraqi threats and demands with what could have been perceived as an Iraqi nuclear threat? Would Israel be forced to cave in to the demands of Iraq because of nuclear blackmail?

It was argued that if there were a four- to five-year lag before Iraq actually did have the bomb, and if that time were used for diplomacy, it would only put Israel in a trap.

If they waited too long to be sure Iraq actually possessed nuclear weapons capability, could they then take the chance of a raid, and—in the face of world opinion—be totally isolated and branded as barbarians for destroying a nuclear reactor and spreading radiation throughout Iraq and the Middle East?

Should it matter whether Iraq could build a bomb in one or two years or five years or ten years?

What difference should it make how long it would take to build a bomb? Shouldn't the facts that they had the capability and the determination to destroy Israel be the only things that counted?

Should Israel be able to declare itself the sole arbiter of who can and who cannot develop atomic weapons in the Middle East?

Shouldn't this greater danger of proliferated atomic bomb know-how created by the merchandising activities of money-first governments like France, Italy and Portugal be of concern worldwide?

Should some backward territory, where checks and balances don't always work and signals are liable to be confused, be able to start a major nuclear conflagration that could destroy entire populations and contaminate huge areas of the earth's surface with dense radioactive fallout?

Would this affect oil deliveries to the rest of the world?

If Israel should obliterate one such source of potential calamity, even if for selfish purposes, wouldn't it be providing a service for the human race?

Was it legal for a sovereign state to create, with the aid of other sovereign states, an instrument capable of destroying several hundred thousand Israelis?

If it was, then was it not also legal to halt that fatal process before it reached completion?

Legal considerations played a small part in the decision-making process. Unfortunately, law generally plays an extremely insignificant role in international relations and in attitudes toward the Arab-Israeli war in particular. It has no enforcing power except war.

International law is invoked by enemies and friends when it suits them and otherwise is ignored.

The Israelis expected Iraq to charge that any military action would be illegal, a violation of international law, and would therefore be considered an act of aggression.

The Israelis thought such a reference to international law to be sheer nonsense.

Iraq considered itself to be in a state of war with Israel. It had never agreed to negotiate an armistice or cease-fire and had repeatedly sent troops and warplanes to fight Israel. War is illegal itself, so how could a single act within that war be any more serious than the war itself?

The questions mounted. But they eventually boiled down to five courses of action: (1) accept the fact Iraq might possibly develop a nuclear capability and learn to live with it; (2) turn up the heat on the diplomatic front by placing added diplomatic pressure on the French and Americans to overcome past failures and gain their cooperation to cut off support to Iraq; (3) step up sabotage and clandestine efforts to frighten the providers of technology to stop deliveries and deny Iraq the necessary tools, people, equipment and knowledge to fashion atomic bombs at its facility at Al Tuwaitha; (4) stage an all-out commando raid to destroy the reactor facility; or (5) destroy the reactor with a pinpoint accurate bombing raid by the Israeli Air Force.

An Iraqi atomic bomb attack on Tel Aviv would have caused about 100,000 casualties, said Professor Alvin Radkowsky, former chief scientist of the U.S. Atomic Energy Commission's marine reactors division and now a member of the Tel Aviv and Ben Gurion Universities' nuclear engineering departments.

His estimate was based on the 1946 U.S. atomic bomb tests at Bikini Atoll in which steel-plated unmanned ships remained virtually intact. Radkowsky said Tel Aviv's buildings would have kept the casualty toll to half of what it was in Hiroshima.

At Hiroshima, the intense heat created by the explosion of the uranium 235 "Little Boy" atomic bomb—

which Radkowsky believes the Iraqis could have produced—literally ignited the Japanese city's mostly wooden buildings in a raging firestorm that killed more than 92,000 people in addition to injuring as many.

According to Radkowsky, radiation would not be enough to do much damage in Tel Aviv. Other scientists estimated as many as 100,000 deaths in Tel Aviv and 100,000 injuries. Begin liked to use the 200,000 figure. Whatever count was used, it was awesome.

Wiping out Tel Aviv and Haifa would virtually destroy Israel. The Arabs would probably have left Jerusalem alone since it has religious significance to them as well as to the western world.

Did Israel have any alternative except to take some action? The United States could survive a first nuclear attack and deliver a counterattack. Tiny Israel could not.

All air bases in Israel could be eliminated in a single strike attack. Begin was convinced no Israeli government, or any other government in a similar position, could take the risk that a foe armed with atomic bombs would not use them.

It was argued that Israel with its concentrated small population could not afford to rely on a second strike deterrence capability.

The phrase "Anticipatory Self-Defense" in the Atomic Age was developed. It was defined as being unreasonable for Israel to have to wait until a nuclear attack had already occurred. The inherent right of self-defense is also anticipatory, it was argued, requiring only an immediate danger of attack to initiate a response.

The obvious Israeli answer was to deem it unacceptable to allow Iraq to be able to build nuclear weapons. Israel could not sit idly by.

It was decided that nothing was as important to Israel's survival in the long run as effecting a major setback to the Iraqi nuclear program.

Urgent diplomacy had already failed. How could it succeed in a strong short-run effort if the cast of characters involved were the same? It couldn't.

Israel had tried with France, Italy and the United States to keep the Iraqi nuclear facility from having the ability to create bombs—and it failed. It was obvious that any additional efforts would meet with the same results.

Time and talk would gain nothing and provide defense for Iraq. Waiting could flare up more turbulence and turmoil in Middle East politics, as Israel might find it necessary to take more military actions to keep spreading nuclear weapons out of the hands of other Arab enemy states.

Clandestine operations, although never proven as having been instigated by Israel (but always assumed so), had delayed but failed to stop Iraqi efforts.

Security was too tight inside the compound in Iraq to smuggle in explosives in an attempt to destroy it. Sabotage in France and Italy and intimidation of the foreign reactor work force (Italians and French) at best slowed down construction. But in spite of those efforts, completion of the facility was pretty much on schedule—summer 1981.

A simple process of elimination left no alternatives except a military solution, if Israel did not want any of its enemies to possess nuclear weapons.

Israel accepted the short-term problems that it hoped would create a long-term solution. A commando raid involving air force transports, helicopters and fighters, would be too expensive in casualties and was not assured of success. The fiasco of the complicated U.S. rescue effort of its hostages in Iran was fresh on everyone's mind. There was no need to even attempt such a complex operation where so many things could go wrong.

It became obvious a commando raid was out of the question for many reasons.

—Too many people would be involved.

—Casualties would be enormous.

—The logistics of transporting men and equipment such a distance were too complex.

—Maintaining secrecy to effect such a large surprise attack would be impossible.

—There would be no aircover for the transport planes because the fighters could not get there and back and loiter on station without air-to-air refueling. Israel had no large air-to-air tankers.

—There was no possibility of rescuing the commandos.

—Barbaric treatment of the many men who would probably be captured.

The only logical solution to destroying the plant would be to send in a flight of attack bombers; this would minimize the risk with maximum assurance of destroying the reactor. Begin felt this plan had to be carried out before the reactor went into operation.

After the reactor was fueled and hot, his concern was that it could have blanketed Baghdad with radiation and tens of thousands of innocent residents could have been hurt. Under such circumstances, no government of Israel could contemplate bombing the reactor. With regard to the possible international reaction, the government worked on the worst-case probability, but still concluded that there was little alternative to the attack.

What kind of fallout would there be from the fuel shipped by France already located on site? Did it matter? At most, if hit, it would be minimal if it was not already loaded in the reactor. Would the attack accelerate the arms race in the Middle East? How could it? Wasn't every country doing its level best already to develop and stockpile the finest weapons they were capable of building or purchasing?

Since the development of OPEC, Arab powers had built up a fire power greater than that of all NATO. Some ministers fully anticipated that the Reagan administration would announce a freeze on weapons to Israel, claiming U.S.-purchased aircraft flown on the raid were used for other than self-defense—a violation of the sales agreement.

"If the United States suspends delivery of weapons to

Israel," argued Sharon, "they would only be hurting themselves. In the Middle East, Israel is one of the only barriers against Soviet expansion."

They also expected American condemnation of the raid to be coupled with an announcement to supply AWACS early-warning aircraft to Saudi Arabia—something Israel was very much against. If such a sale were consummated prior to the attack, however, it would be totally impossible for the raid to take place undetected at a later date. At least now there was a chance.

They knew too, that the raid could and probably would undermine Israel's relations with the New French government of François Mitterrand. It could also damage the peace treaty with Egypt.

But a long and hard study decided that nothing was as vital to Israel's survival as delaying the Iraqi nuclear program.

There was consideration for Saddam Hussein's response to the raid. Hussein's military had been sapped in the war with Iran. Eleven of the 12 to 13 Iraqi army divisions were bogged down on the Iranian front. This also included deployment of the 3,000 tanks, 2,500 armored troop carriers and 2,000 cannons.

Since Israel and Iraq do not share a common border, even if Iraq wanted to use the army in retaliation they would have to cross through either Syria or Jordan. Relations between Syria and Iraq were strained. Damascus was helping Iran in the war.

Jordan, although politically close to Iraq, would probably not allow Iraq to cross through their country. Israel had previously told King Hussein of Jordan it would view Iraqi presence within his boundaries as a cause for war.

Iraq had no aircraft that could launch a successful conventional weapon counterattack against Israel's air defenses and the constantly on-alert air force interceptors. Besides, the Iraqi Air Force had a poor showing against Iran, and such a raid on Israel would be too complex for them to pull off.

The Iraqi Army could also fire SCUD missiles. It had 12 launchers and one SCUD model with a range of about 275 miles, more than the distance from the Iraqi-Jordanian border to the Mediterranean. However, the SCUD was an inaccurate missile and intelligence said the missiles were not currently deployed along the border.

Israeli leadership concurred no counterattack would be sent. Hussein's real area of retaliation would be twofold: Launch terrorist attacks against Israel and mobilize world opinion against Israel at the United Nations.

Israel felt it had little chance in the Third World-dominated United Nations anyway and really wasn't too concerned about it. With the exception of declaring Israel a state in 1948, the United Nations had basically been a hostile organization toward the Jews. But in the world press, they were willing to take their chances that the truth would blunt any serious actions against Israel.

After all, no other Arab country including Syria, Saudia Arabia, Egypt and Jordan wanted to be under the threat of Iraq's nuclear power either. Other leaders realized the unreliable, unstable and unsavory regime in Iraq could not be trusted with nuclear weapons.

The feeling was the Arab countries might stick together on the surface and pay lip service to denouncing Israeli "aggression," but deep down the Israeli leaders expected some relieved feelings among their Arab neighbors.

There had been a western world fever of protest pushing for nuclear disarmament and mass demonstrations against the peaceful use of nuclear energy throughout Europe, Japan and North America. Protesting included eliminating the use of nuclear power stations on the grounds they might inadvertently or accidentally leak radiation. This concern could help Israel's cause.

What about news of the raid? Should Israel release the news? What if there were heavy casualties? If they didn't release the information, it was feared Israel would be cited as admitting the actions were illegal.

News of the attack would need to be released promptly. It would be impossible to keep it a secret—especially if there were prisoners. It was decided to withhold information until Iraq broke the news first.

What would Israel gain from the raid?

Three things: (1) they would gain time by setting the Iraqi nuclear program back at least three years; (2) they would send a clear message to their enemies that Israel's military capability is undiminished; and (3) they would send an indirect warning to foreign sources of nuclear technology such as France and Italy to stop supplying the Arabs.

One popular remark heard during the debates reflected much of the mood: "If I have a choice of being popular and dead, or unpopular and alive, I'll choose alive."

The comment of one leader was, "Why should we tolerate a viper out to harm us anyway? What do we have to lose by pulling its fangs?"

At a secret meeting in October 1980, the Israeli Cabinet voted to back up Begin's fateful decision to attack the Iraqi reactor. Only the details of timing and operational details of the air attack were left to a select committee of three.

11

Hot Date Intelligence

As DEBATE RAGED in Israel, Mossad agents and military intelligence quietly but feverishly kept track of progress on the reactor.

The more they learned, the more intensely they concentrated on the project. They worked together and coordinated their information skillfully.

Military intelligence is the larger of the two operations and specializes in collecting and analyzing data involving Arab states adjacent to Israel, military-oriented intelligence and all national security intelligence.

Mossad's U.S. counterpart is the CIA. It is largely an overseas covert organization.

In spite of the sabotage in France, scare tactics in Italy, and the political pressure in the United States, the reactor was on schedule—and nearing completion.

In the spring and summer of 1980, Israeli intelligence notified the prime minister that they expected the plant to be fueled with uranium and to become radioactive as early as July or at the latest, September 1981.

Begin shuddered.

French nuclear scientists aiding the Iraqis communicated to Israeli intelligence that they expected to have the reactor operational by September, but the Iraqis were "pressing them" to advance the date to July.

This created uncertainty between a July or September date.

If action were to be taken by the Israeli leadership group's own ground rules, it had to be taken prior to the possible spread of any radioactivity.

Israel had projected that the Iraqis would not be able to produce nuclear weapons before 1985. (A date with which the CIA agreed.)

It was immaterial whether they could make weapons by 1981 or 1982 or 1985 if the Israeli government was committed to no damage to the plant after it became radioactive.

Tension mounted in the government. The time for decision as to what action to take was at hand.

The fuse was lit.

12

Continuous Warnings

DEBATING, PLANNING, GATHERING intelligence were all going on feverishly behind the scenes.

But Israel made a conscious effort to be certain there were continuous public warnings of severe consequences in an effort to stall construction of Iraq's nuclear plant.

There were the saboteurs on April 6, 1979, that blew up the warehouse in La Seyne-sur-Mer. The intense Israeli pressure on the United States and France. The quiet diplomatic efforts by the United States to convince the French to stop the construction in Iraq. The death of Egyptian Professor Yahia al-Meshad, the physicist who headed Iraq's nuclear program. The anonymous and threatening letters sent to technicians working on the project mailed both in their native countries and from Iraq to give the perception that threatening danger was nearby. There was Begin's speech given specifically on France's National Day—July 14, 1980—in which he accused France of "creating an extremely dangerous situation."

That same day, Deputy Prime Minister Yigael Yadin said "Israel would take measures against the atomic program."

Some believed these were Israeli bluffs. But in the past such warnings always carried a sting.

Israel sent representatives to Europe and the United

States to try to interest newspapers and television networks in the issue.

Prime Minister Begin activated a campaign of secret diplomacy that included personal letters to the French and other European heads of state in an effort to persuade them to cut off support for the project. The tactic worked in at least one country—The Netherlands. But the French and Italians continued to turn a deaf ear.

A lot of press was generated in July 1980, through the Israeli efforts. The message was there—the Iraqi reactor was a matter of life or death to Israel, and tiny Israel would do what was necessary to prevent the spread of nuclear devices to the Arab world.

Throughout the entire warning process, the Israelis never directly said they would attack. One had to read between the lines to see the threat was there.

On July 28, 1980, Foreign Minister Yitshak Shamir called in the Charge d'Affaires (the number two man) at the French Embassy in Israel to express the government's feelings on the matter. And once again Shamir was not a happy man.

Shamir gave another warning in an August 11, 1980, *Time* magazine interview: "The Iraqi nuclear reactor may ignite conflict in this region and cancel the efforts to reach peace."

Even *Time*'s reporter commented, "Israel had given a silent warning that if she considered Iraq close to reaching the bomb, she might use a preemptive strike on Iraq's facility."

How could the warning be any clearer?

On the eve of August 7, 1980, a small bomb exploded near the front door of the unoccupied home of the manager of the Italian firm SNIA Techint which was building the "hot cells" for the reactor facility. At the same time, two bombs exploded at the company offices in Rome. There was damage in both places but no injuries.

However, a message was getting through from some

unidentified group. In Rome it was called "The Committee to Safeguard the Islamic Revolution."

A message was left behind in the SNIA Techint manager's apartment: "We know about your personal collaboration with the enemies of the Islamic Revolution. All those who cooperate with our enemies will be our enemies."

The message demanded an end to the firm's help of the Iraqis. It concluded: "If you don't do this, we will strike out against you and your family without pity."

Italian police never got proof of who made the threats, but the Mossad was again at the top of the suspect list.

Security around the workers on the project tightened, but work continued. However, Italians now realized that it was dangerous work.

Another blunt alarm was sounded by Israel Deputy Defense Minister Mordechai Zippori in August 1980: "We will explore all legal and humane avenues. If pressure doesn't work, we'll have to consider other means," he said.

French President François Mitterrand received a report from three eminent scientists before the raid. After 2,000 words it concluded that France had given Iraq the capability to produce one atomic bomb a year.

When Secretary of State Alexander Haig visited Israel during his April 1981 trip to the Middle East, Foreign Minister Yitshak Shamir raised the subject without going into details. But it was on the agenda and Haig was aware of the concern.

In Washington late in 1980, the Defense Intelligence Agency told the White House: "Prudently, we must assume that Israel is considering some sort of action to forestall Iraqi acquisition of a nuclear capability, and we must consider the implications of such actions."

With prophetic accuracy the report predicted: "The most pressing problem for the United States is not the prospect of a nuclear conflict involving Israel and Iraq, but rather the prospect of a preemptive Israeli strike with conventional weapons against the reactor."

In March 1981 on the floor of the U.S. Senate, Sen. Alan Cranston of California warned: "This massive Iraqi nuclear development program is under way despite the fact that Iraq has no parallel program for developing commercial nuclear power.

"In fact, I have been informed . . . that in the absence of any associated power program, a weapons capability is clearly the option the Iraqis are pursuing."

Cranston continued, "Iraq is trying to use its oil power to blackmail other nations into supplying nuclear weapons technology—threatening a destabilizing arms race in the region.

"There is no evidence that actual bomb design has been done in Iraq, but Iraq is demonstrating graphically the danger that radical oil powers will use the 'oil weapon' to blackmail other nations into imprudent sales of sensitive nuclear technology and cooperation in its use.

"According to the authoritative assessment, the Iraqis are embarked on a Manhattan Project-type approach. They are pursuing all avenues which could provide them with a capability to produce nuclear explosives," he concluded.

During Senate hearings, Cranston also said he had evidence that the IAEA's last inspection of the Osirak reactor had been conducted by flashlight and that critical fuel elements were locked in a vault out of view.

Inspections every six months meant little. The Iraqis could shut down the reactor and secretly remove its plutonium in as little as three months after it began operation. After that, it starts to be contaminated by isotopes of plutonium that are not as effective in weapons.

Cranston estimated Iraq could produce enough plutonium to build three bombs a year. The State Department challenged the claim and estimated Iraq could only make one bomb a year. The Israelis really didn't care how many could be built, but that they could be built at all.

Iraq's efforts got President Jimmy Carter's attention.

Carter, a former naval officer who passed Admiral Rickover's personal scrutiny to become a member of the elite nuclear Navy, understood nuclear power plants.

He was so worried he made a variety of frantic behind-the-scenes intercessions to block the Iraqi progress. Carter asked Italy to reconsider its sale of the "hot cells" which could be used to separate bomb-grade plutonium. The Italians refused, but did agree to place a team of technicians at the Osirak site to try and ensure Iraq did not perform the separation process.

Carter also was disturbed about Iraq's attempt to purchase from Canada, West Germany and the United States ten tons of depleted uranium fuel that could be used to make plutonium.

According to Thomas O'Toole of the *Washington Post,* Carter won from the French, in three extraordinary approaches to French President Valéry Giscard d'Estaing, an agreement to preirradiate the highly enriched uranium fuel so it would be "poisoned," making it more difficult for Iraq to divert it from research to an atomic weapon.

Carter also persuaded Giscard to sign a contract with Iraq that called for the presence of 150 French technicians at the Osirak reactor until at least 1989 to ensure Iraq did not develop a bomb.

"Both these agreements were unique in the world of nuclear power," a source close to the Carter administration said. "They would not have happened except for Carter's intervention."

The sale of the ten tons of uranium didn't go through, in part because Canada squelched the deal before the United States was consulted. Canada balked because there appeared to be no good reason Iraq would want depleted uranium, except to irradiate it to make plutonium.

"You can argue that you'd use depleted uranium as a shielding material or as a training material for technicians learning to handle radioactive materials, but it's a very weak argument," one source said. "At the time, it sounded like an even weaker argument for Iraq to want to buy the stuff."

Under secretary of state Joseph Sisco, a central figure in U.S. Middle East policy for over a decade, was later to summarize U.S. government involvement over the Voice of America, when he said the United States made serious efforts to persuade the French not to sell Iraq enriched weapons-grade uranium.

"We tried to convince them to sell Iraq a form of uranium that could not be converted into weapons. We failed."

The continuous warnings were having no impact.

"We warned the French, we warned the Italians, we warned the Americans not to supply the equipment to the Iraqis. My conscience is clear in ordering the attack," Begin was to say in a post-attack news conference.

13

The Decision and Politics

IMMEDIATELY FOLLOWING THE secret October 1980 Cabinet
meeting (the date of which is still classified), during
which a bombing attack against the reactor was agreed
upon, Israeli Defense Forces Commander Raphael
("Raful") Eitan quickly ordered the air force to begin
preparations and training for the maximum range low-
level bombing attack against Iraq. They had already been
training in low-level, long-range flights since the F-16
arrived in Israel.

Once the debate had ended, a decision on when to
attack the reactor was necessary. Begin favored swift,
decisive action.

He started to meet with his closest advisers on sched-
uling the attack. The three, who all shared his ideas, were
Ariel Sharon, Minister of Agriculture and close political
ally of Begin; Rafael "Raful" Eitan, Chief of Staff (or
commander) of the Israeli Defense Forces; and Foreign
Minister Yitzhak Shamir.

The frequent deliberations of this group were kept
secret from the rest of the Cabinet, the Knesset, the
opposition, and any foreign countries, including the
United States and Egypt.

They scheduled the raid for November 1980.

But events beyond Begin's control were to change that
date.

On September 17, 1980, Iraq canceled the 1975 agreement with Iran over the Shatt-al-Arab estuary that separated the two neighbors at the top of the Persian Gulf, and war began.

There was also conflict over the oil-rich Khuzistan area of Iran.

On September 20, fighting began to accelerate. By September 22, the fighting assumed major proportions with full-scale air attacks from Iraq against Iran including Tehran. On September 25, Iraq offered Iran terms for a complete armistice—which amounted to surrender for Iran. It was rejected and both countries started raiding each other's oil-producing facilities with a vengeance.

The Israeli Chief of Military Intelligence, Aluf Yehoshua Saguy, appeared on Israeli television on September 28, wondering out loud why the Iranians had not bombed the Iraqi nuclear installations. Or was it a suggestion?

On September 30, two Iranian F-4 Phantom jet fighter-bombers struck and bombed the Iraqi nuclear reactor in Al Tuwaitha. The bombs did not hit the main buildings and damage was minor.

Begin had mixed reactions to this raid. He was disappointed the Iranians hadn't done the job right to save him the trouble, yet he had confidence and pride in his own air force and would be reassured of a job well done if they did it—even at the risk of some of their lives.

It wasn't long before it was obvious that the war between Iraq and Iran would drag on, and as danger mounted France and Italy evacuated most of their 150 to 200 technicians from Iraq.

As Israeli intelligence analyzed developments, it was assumed work on the reactor would be stopped for the duration of the war, or possibly indefinitely. With work at a standstill and the reactor of no threat or danger to Israel, Begin canceled the November attack. However, the air force continued to train.

The war with Iran was planned by Hussein to be

lightning swift and immediately decisive. Much to his disgust, it bogged down into a long-term World War I-type conflict, with massive numbers of front-line troops facing each other across trenches. Casualties were enormous. There were sporadic air attacks.

As it stabilized, the French and Italian technicians returned in late February 1981. Work started again—at an accelerated pace. Since construction was now going to continue, Begin and his advisers scheduled an attack for the end of February 1981. Deputy Prime Minister Yigael Yadin voiced stiff objection. He continued to argue with Begin and Begin yielded. The date was postponed.

A third date was set in March, but now Israel was getting bogged down in the crisis in Lebanon. Again, plans for the attack had to be shelved.

The next date for the strike was set for Sunday, May 10. Begin intended to stick to it.

But word of the raid was leaking out.

On the evening of May 9, opposition party leader and political opponent in the upcoming June 30 elections, Shimon Péres, learned the attack was planned for the next day.

He had been of the plan "in principle," but now he knew the specific date.

Under Premiers David Ben Gurion and Levy Eshkol, Péres had been one of the movers and shakers behind construction of Israel's nuclear reactors at Nahal Sorek and Dimona between 1958 and 1965.

He was also a friend of François Mitterrand, the socialist running for the presidency in the French elections being held the very day the attack was scheduled. Mitterrand had campaigned against President Giscard d'Estaing's policy of supplying Iraq with so much nuclear technology.

Péres felt, if elected, Mitterrand would move to increase safeguards and controls over Iraq's French reactor, possibly terminating most of the accord.

With the raid scheduled just hours away, Péres wrote Begin a vaguely worded "Personal and Top Secret" note, saying it was "not desirable" to bomb the reactor at this time. He argued that Mitterrand would win and there were indications the new French president would do everything possible to make the Iraqi reactor impotent, militarily. He warned Begin that the raid would leave Israel as isolated "as a lonely shrub in the desert."

The text read as follows:

May 10
Personal and Top Secret
Mr. Prime Minister:

At the end of December 1980 you called me into your office in Jerusalem and told me about a certain extremely serious matter. You did not solicit to my response and I myself (despite my instinctive feeling) did not respond in the circumstances that then existed.

I feel this morning that it is my supreme civic duty to advise you, after serious consideration and in weighing the national interest, to desist from this thing.

I speak as a man of experience. The deadlines reported by us (and I well understand our people's anxiety) are not the realistic deadlines. Material can be changed for (other) material. And what is intended to prevent can become a catalyst.

On the other hand Israel would be like a tree in the desert—and we also have that to be concerned about.

I add my voice—and it is not mine alone—to the voices of those who tell you not to do it, and certainly not at the present time in the present circumstances.

Respectfully,
Shimon Péres

It was an esoteric letter and, if it fell into the wrong hands, the content would be hard to decipher.

"Material can be exchanged for material" meant that Mitterrand, if elected, might be persuaded to substitute low-grade uranium for the weapons-grade uranium France was supplying to Iraq.

The phrasing "what is intended to prevent can become a catalyst" was meant to hint to Begin that an Israeli air attack on the reactor might spur the Arab world to make even greater efforts to obtain nuclear weapons.

The next paragraph meant to warn Begin that an air action would leave Israel isolated from the rest of the world. The phrase, "we also have that to be concerned about," referred to Israel's own nuclear program and Péres' fears the Iraqi attack might focus world attention on Israel's nuclear capability—not especially helpful to Israel.

The logic of waiting on the French election was hard to argue with. Meanwhile, down at the Etzion air base near Elat, a group of young Israeli fighter pilots having just finished their lengthy briefing for the flight, quietly preflighted their F-16s and carefully checked the attached bombs.

Sworn to secrecy about their destination, they climbed into their cockpits and were sitting at the end of the long, hot runway with their jet engines whining, methodically checking a cockpit full of dials and gauges as the minutes ticked away, waiting for the exact predetermined time to take off.

Begin huddled with Sharon, Eitan and Shamir. The decision was made. The raid would be scrubbed until after the French elections.

Eitan grabbed a nearby phone and called air force operations. Just minutes before takeoff, Etzion control tower broke radio silence and ordered the puzzled pilots to shut down their engines while the aircraft were de-armed.

Péres' letter was destined to create a firestorm of controversy between two intense competitors for the reins of power in Israel. Ugly, hard feelings would later publicly erupt.

Was Péres opposed to the raid only on the day of the French elections, or was he opposed to the raid at any time?

Begin claimed Péres had pretended to oppose the action on French election day, whereas in truth, he had opposed the action altogether. Péres, on the other hand, contended it was his position that he objected to military action before "exhausting the diplomatic option" with the possible new French government.

Begin said Péres' letter was intended as a "double insurance policy." If the operation failed, he would have said he had been against it all along; if it had succeeded, he would have said (and indeed did say) that he was only opposed to the specific May 10 timing.

Israel's leadership in the know waited. But they didn't have long to wait. Mitterrand won the election.

Hope against hope, Begin now wished that France's newly elected president would denounce and terminate the Iraqi nuclear project.

In early June, France's Foreign Minister Claude Cheysson said that his country would not engage in future nuclear deals like they did with Iraq, but that they would honor existing commitments.

Péres was disappointed and Begin felt his previous actions were justified. The die was cast for Israeli military action. Everything else had failed.

Even if France cut off its supply of uranium to the Iraqi reactor, Begin felt Baghdad would have been able to operate the plant with uranium procured elsewhere. Begin made the final decision and issued the orders June 4 for the Sunday, June 7 attack.

Begin had a scheduled meeting with Egyptian President Anwar Sadat at Ophira, formerly known as Sharm-el-Sheikh, on the very southern tip of the Sinai. It was a colorful ceremonial meeting in which the Egyptian president had come to examine the territory he was to get in 1982 as part of the Camp David peace process. The territory included virtually all of the Sinai Peninsula, including some Jewish settlements, and the air base from which the air strike, unknown to him, would be launched in three days.

At the meeting, Sadat was making an effort to influence Begin to exercise restraint in the Syrian crisis that had arisen over the placement by Damascus of ground-to-air missiles in southern Lebanon. Begin had declared this move to be a threat to peace and had even announced he was going to destroy the missiles, subject to efforts by the Americans to have them removed. Sadat thought this action could lead to another war and didn't want his country dragged into it. Rather, he wanted to keep the Camp David peace process moving with autonomy talks for the Palestinians.

Sadat felt increasingly isolated from the Arab world at this time because of his peace with Israel, and at least wanted to get something for it. Begin wasn't going to give him any feeling of relief about his isolation. He wanted to keep Sadat on a political tightrope.

Meeting with the president of Egypt just three days before the raid would give the Arab world the perception of Egyptian involvement, although Sadat was completely unaware of what was about to happen.

The suspicious Arab world would assume collusion between Egypt and Israel and as a result continue to keep Egypt isolated.

Besides, in 11 months Egypt was scheduled to regain the rest of the Sinai. Although they would be furious about the raid, they wouldn't take any action to jeopardize repossession of their lost territory.

This isolation of Egypt from the Arab world was a great benefit to Israel since peace with Egypt kept them from worrying about a pincer attack, which allowed Israel to concentrate its military forces along its eastern and northern borders.

Begin was a cagey, calculating politician. Self-defense was one thing. Politics was another.

Although rising in the polls, Begin realized there were political ramifications to the raid this close to the June 30 Israeli elections.

The hot-date scare of a radioactive reactor in early July was one of Begin's concerns. He was also paranoid that if he should lose the election at the end of June, winner Péres would never have the "guts" to initiate such a strike and Israel would live forever with an Iraqi nuclear threat.

Valuable time passed while waiting to see what the French government would do. Begin was getting boxed in as he waited and the June 30 elections drew nearer.

Hot-date intelligence kept saying the reactor could be hot within days after the election. This was a new urgency.

Begin was determined that no stroke could take place after the elections. Regardless how they went, there would be a transition period before the swearing in of the next government, and such a transition government would not have a mandate from the people for an action as wide-ranging as the attack.

The early polls showed Begin behind, but later his party was in the lead.

Another major political concern had to do with if the raid failed or a plane was shot down and a pilot was taken prisoner. Any electoral benefits could be neutralized or work in reverse.

For nine months Begin had been living with the idea of destroying Iraq's nuclear weapon capability. Now the pressure was mounting. The date was set and there was no turning back.

Begin's—and much of Israel's—destiny was trusted to a few select pilots.

Begin asked Eitan how they would refer to the attack. Eitan quoted Biblical verses from Jeremiah 50 and 51: "The noise of battle is in the land, the noise of great destruction. Before your eyes I will repay Babylon and all who live in Babylonia for all the wrong they have done in Zion, declares the Lord."

Firmly and emphatically Eitan told the prime minister of Israel, "We will call it Operation Babylon."

14

Planning and Preparation

Dov RETURNED TO his squadron puzzled. He got out his calculator and figured the maximum range of the F-16 to be 580 miles.

He then looked at a Middle East wall map and stretched a string out from his base at Ramat David and drew a 600-mile arc.

He couldn't figure out any plausible target at the maximum range. He thought to himself the target must be somewhere in northern Syria.

For the moment, he was a squadron commander without planes. He set up a syllabus for training new pilots and spent his time figuring out low-level navigation techniques and routes and how to squeeze more miles out of the F-16 fuel load.

When Dan and his group finished training in Utah, the first four F-16s were ferried to Israel by U.S. Air Force pilots with temporary U.S. markings on the planes. When they arrived, training intensified.

Most combat fights in Israel are less than an hour long. When Israeli fighters take off in a combat situation, as soon as they go "wheels up," the pilots immediately turn on armament switches. Within two minutes they can be engaging MIGs.

It's 68 miles to Damascus from Ramat David, so long flights just aren't part of the Israeli fighter pilot's regimen.

It took a lot of retraining in the skills of maximum-endurance flying for an Israeli pilot to convince himself to remain airborne for nearly three hours. On practice flights, the pilots would stare in amazement when they reached the halfway point and their inertial navigation system (INS) read 600 miles back to base.

The IAF has always respected the U.S. Navy's skill in this area of maximum range and low fuel BINGO, or the ability to return to the carrier with just enough fuel for a couple of landing passes before the fuel tanks run dry.

The planes were ferried to Israel with only wing tanks, so up through the winter of 1980-81 Israel had no 300-gallon centerline tanks. That left the planes about 25 minutes or 375 miles short of making the round-trip to Baghdad. But the tanks were on order, although no one knew when they would arrive.

A tiny country, Israel is 210 miles long and 45 miles wide and is about the size of Massachusetts. At the time of Operation Babylon preparations, it still possessed the Sinai Peninsula captured from Egypt in 1967 which wasn't scheduled for return to Egypt as part of the Camp David peace process until April 1982. The Sinai is a vast desert area that gave the IAF plenty of room for low-level navigation practice.

Though they gradually learned to pace their diet and remain in the cockpit for extended periods, getting used to the long flights created humorous incidents for the pilots. One such incident occurred when a wingman of Dan's landed at Ramat David after being strapped in his plane six hours. He got to the end of the runway, pulled off on the taxiway, and stopped his F-16 with blue smoke coming from his skidding tires. He shut down his engine, jumped down from the cockpit, and ran from the plane. Thinking the aircraft was on fire, Dan quickly called the emergency crews. At the edge of the taxiway, the pilot ripped off his flight suit and squatted down. The only thing required of the fire crews when they arrived on the scene minutes later was to bring some toilet paper for the embarrassed fighter jock.

Five more F-16s were delivered in September along with the final four planes that had been in Utah for training.

In late September, three pilots, Dov, Dan and Isaac, the wing and base commander at Ramat David, met with the operational planning chief of the air force. For the first time, he shared with the three leaders the target to be destroyed.

At this point the only people privy to the target information were a small unit of top IAF headquarters operational planners and now the three pilots. The other pilots would not know the destination until the preflight briefing for the canceled May 10 flight.

The pilots were flabbergasted. They had never dreamed of going to Iraq as they practiced their low-level navigation. It was to be the longest mission in the history of the IAF. The previous record was set during strikes to the Aswan area of Egypt during the 1969-71 War of Attrition.

Decisions now had to be made—how to plan the attack, the types of weapons to be used, procedures, implementation of intelligence, navigation courses to avoid detection, time of day, best angles of attack to destroy the reactor, how many planes to use to ensure destruction and hundreds of other details.

Technical experts pored over plans, ideas, handbooks and philosophies before it all fell into place.

Dov's squadron was selected to fly the mission and, because of his past experience and expertise, Dan would also fly on the raid.

The attack was expected to take place in November 1980.

Dan wasn't happy. He felt because of the significance of the raid and its impact on IAF history, the attack should be flown by both F-16 squadrons—Dov's and his. He made repeated trips by light aircraft from Ramat David in northern Israel down to Air Force Headquarters in Tel Aviv, banging on the doors of any of the privileged few decision-makers involved to try to persuade them that his squadron should also be involved.

Finally, one day the persistent pilot was virtually thrown out of the headquarters compound with: "Okay, okay, you're in, you're in, relax. Your squadron will be part of the raid." He was one excited young man flying back to his base.

Targeting discussions between the pilots, operational staff and intelligence experts were held to coordinate the raid. The planning was meticulous.

Blueprints of the facility at Al Tuwaitha were clandestinely obtained. Physicists and other scientists studied them to determine precisely the best location to drop the bombs to render the reactor useless. They figured all the installations at the plant were worthless without the reactor. The size of the cupola was measured to determine the best size of bombs to use.

There was some discussion about the use of so-called "smart bombs," which are actually GBU-15 and made by Rockwell International. These bombs can be dropped from the attacking airplanes some distance from the target and, through the use of remote-controlled movable fins on the bombs and a television camera in the nose of the bomb, are steered to a target through sophisticated data-link equipment transmitted to the airplane cockpit. Such a bombing technique has the advantage of keeping the bombing aircraft away from the dangerous SAM and AAA threat, but also has more chances for something to go wrong.

With a target where accuracy must be 100 percent on the first pass, simple 2,000-pound MK 84 "dumb" bombs would be the safest and most effective.

"You can have smart planes and dumb bombs, or dumb planes and smart bombs, but you don't need both smart planes and smart bombs," according to a fighter pilot expression.

Israeli F-16s are smart planes.

Planners of the raid also felt 2,000-pound slick bombs

would best penetrate the cupola and do the most damage. The pilots felt most comfortable keeping things simple—that makes for the most effective and failproof system of delivery.

Extra care was taken in handling the bombs. "Slick" bombs meant that every inch of the fins was checked for bumps, dents, dings, bends or any small telltale alterations that could affect airflow of the bomb that could throw accuracy off 10 to 15 feet.

The MK 84 produces blast, fragmentation and deep cratering effects and can have instantaneous or delayed fusing. The fragmentation envelope rises to 2,800 feet in nine seconds after the bomb explodes, then it falls to 1,000 feet at 22 seconds and disappears in 27 seconds. It extends horizontally for 3,400 feet.

Checking and cross-checking continued.

To get confirmation that the MK 84s would do the job, Israeli scientists met with structural specialists from the U.S. Nuclear Regulatory Commission (NRC). The NRC, which regulates and issues licenses for nuclear energy uses, protects the public health, safety and environment in the United States.

The meeting took place October 9, 1980, and involved Israeli doctors Joseph Kivity and Joseph Saltovitz who were engineers at Technion University in Haifa. They met with John O'Brien, James Costello and Shou Hou of the NRC's research office in Washington. According to a NRC memo on the meeting, the men discussed the dynamic response of reactor subsystems to explosions within the reactor containment building.

The memo stated the Israeli scientists "clearly defined" that the threat they wanted U.S. experts to assess was "what would happen if a 1,000 kilogram (2,200-pound) charge penetrates concrete barriers and detonates after penetration."

The memo continued: "Because of a lack of real interest in underground siting as a protective measure against sabotage it was unclear whether the Israelis were interested in defending their own plants or destroying someone else's."

The meeting also had a "discussion focused on identifying vulnerable safety systems whose failure might have significant consequences and optimal targets for sabotage."

The meeting was quietly set up without the usual U.S. State Department coordination.

"The Israeli Embassy was asked to arrange the meeting for the Israeli Electric Company, who supposedly was making inquiries about the safety of a civilian power reactor Israel was considering buying from the United States and had nothing to do with what happened in Iraq," Israeli Embassy spokesman Avi Pazner told *Washington Post* correspondent George C. Wilson after the raid.

Selection of the type of bombs to be used led the rest of the planning progress. The decision to use "slick" bombs gave the F-16 the "go" as the plane to be used. The next consideration was determining the best airplane dive angle in which to demolish the target as the planes attacked the reactor. The dive angle was also part of the bomb-fusing problem. If the planes came zooming in at virtual ground level, surprise would be total, but the released bombs could hit the dome concrete and steel cupola and ricochet off without destroying the reactor.

There was also concern about the fragmentation pattern of the bombs—the distance and altitude an exploding bomb would blast shrapnel when it detonated. A pilot could blow himself or his buddies out of the sky if they dove too low or too closely behind a plane dropping bombs. The frag or bomb blast pattern is 2,800 feet after nine seconds. It would be lethal for any following plane to follow too closely or too low.

With this in mind, and to have a greater destructive explosion, there were thoughts to have all bombs with delayed fuses so they would explode together after the last plane dropped its bombs into the dome. That would put real pressure on all pilots to perform precisely during the attack.

An additional benefit of delayed fusing was that the target wouldn't be obscured to the rest of the flight after the lead plane dropped its bombs and they exploded, causing dust and debris.

On the other hand, the gun cameras in each following plane in the attack couldn't record any intelligence to see just what damage was done.

The decision was made to use fuses with just enough delay to allow the bomb to penetrate the reactor dome before exploding.

Dive angles of 10 degrees, 20 degrees, 30 degrees and 40 degrees were considered. All dive angles offered a risk to the pilots from SAMs and blistering anti-aircraft fire (AAA).

But this mission was designed for results first and pilot safety second. For the F-16 to come downward towards the target at a 30- to 45-degree angle meant the best chance of the bomb penetrating the concrete and steel cupola and exploding inside to destroy the reactor core.

Actually, if the airplane dive angle was 30 degrees, the impact angle of the bomb would be 44 to 66 degrees, because once the bomb left the plane and headed for the ground, gravity would pull it down steeper.

In a bombing mission, there are seven specific points or times that must be planned in order to drop the bomb accurately.

1. Pop-up Point—Up until now, the pilot has been navigating to the target, hugging the ground to avoid radar detection. Now he must select a fast air speed, go into afterburner for extra thrust, set a climb angle by pulling the nose of the airplane up 45 degrees into the air, and visually spot the target. He is now about four miles from the target, heading in the opposite direction he'll be going as he leaves the target area.

2. Pull-down Altitude—The predetermined altitude where the pilot works the controls to turn the plane 90 degrees and aim it toward the target. The pilot's eyes

remain fixed on the target at this point. All the information he needs is on the HUD in front of him.

3. Apex Altitude—The actual altitude and point the plane soars up to before the changes in the controls take effect that start heading the plane for the ground. This altitude is important to know so the pilot doesn't spend more time exposed to SAMs and AAA than is necessary to complete the job.

4. Tracking Time on Final—The apex altitude should be figured so there are only three to five seconds for the pilot to get the plane's bombsight lined up and stabilized on the target as he comes down toward it to release the bombs. That way the pilot has minimum exposure to ground fire.

5. Release Point—After tracking on final, the altitude at which the bombsight must be lined up so the pipper on the bombsight is on the target and indicates the instant the bombs must be pickled off the plane by the pilot to ensure an accurate hit of the target. Instantly, after the bomb releases, the pilot starts to pull up to escape.

6. Recovery Altitude—This is the lowest possible altitude to the target the plane flies to ensure a safe escape. There is settling or sinking of the aircraft because of the fraction-of-a-second delay in response to aircraft control movement after the release point. This altitude is computed to be the lowest altitude a plane can fly without the threat of being knocked out of the sky by shrapnel from the exploding bomb blast dropped by the plane in front.

7. Escape Maneuver and Heading—To defeat any SAM missiles, the pilot must quickly maneuver the plane in different directions using sometimes up to seven to eight G's and 90-degree out-of-plane turns while egressing for home with the afterburner thundering and spitting out a tongue of flame as the plane streaks for the safety of high altitude.

If the pilot does it right, the heat-seeking missiles fired at him will be defeated and won't be able to dart up the tail of the fighter-bomber and destroy it.

Anything that makes it more difficult for AAA gunners to see, such as flying into the sun, is a bonus that fits in with this planning too.

Once the type of bombs and impact angles were determined, the planners simply figured the final attack phase of the flight backwards.

As the Israeli planners backed up the profile for dropping bombs, they dug into books as thick as New York telephone directories with computer-figured charts, tables and graphs to determine the recovery altitudes. Each of the other ingredients for a successful bomb drop would be figured from that altitude.

A 2,000-pound bomb has a frag pattern that reaches 2,400 feet into the air on a 30-degree dive. From there, the release point is figured, which would back up three to five seconds tracking on final time at 480 knots, which would then figure the apex altitude, which is determined by the pull-down altitude, which is determined by how high the pilot goes from the pull-up point.

With the bomb exploding deep in the reactor, the frag pattern could be reduced as much as 50 percent.

The Israeli pilots practiced and practiced and practiced so they could handle the mission so swiftly that their apex was less than 5,000 feet above the ground and they could virtually drop the bombs with their eyes closed. Of course, that was without the threat of enemy ground fire and fighters in the air. Surprise and professionalism were the keys for success.

The secrecy of this mission was vital to its success. The pilots needed that precious 30 seconds of surprise to be able to drop the first bombs to destroy the target before the Iraqi gunners and missile operators could get their weapon systems operating to shoot down the incoming F-16s.

They mostly practiced with BDU 33s, a 33-pound dummy practice bomb that simulates real bombs and explodes with white phosphorous smoke so pilot and ground monitoring personnel can visually tell how close to the target they hit. There were a few practice flights dropping live MK 84 2,000-pound bombs on a desert target, but not many.

Although none of the pilots in the flight, except the three leaders, would know the actual target location until the preflight brief, they all practiced dive-bombing targeting on an Israeli radar dome site in the Negev. It realistically portrayed the reactor dome. Some press reports said a practice reactor was built for them on which to practice. But this was not the case. That could have compromised the mission to snoopy U.S. or Soviet satellites flying overhead.

As the weeks and months of practice wore on, the pilots honed their skills. They practiced 30- to 45-degree dive angles and artfully reduced required tracking time from five to three seconds. Because of the close aircraft interval required on roll in, it was demanding work.

This meant a recovery altitude of 3,800 feet to avoid bomb fragments and less exposure to SAMs and AAA fire. The U.S. Air Force usually allows a 500-foot safety factor or cushion for error in frag pattern calculations. The Israelis decided to press the attack right to the minimums with no built-in safety factor. The muffling effect on the bombs because they would explode inside the dome would be the Israelis' safety factor.

The best threat provided by an air defense system against invading aircraft is to force the enemy to recognize their attacking forces don't have air superiority.

The ground-controlled SAM and AAA weapons must be so threatening to incoming aircraft an enemy won't even use fighters or bombers because they realize the losses would be unacceptable. That it would be nothing less than a suicide mission.

The Israeli pilots on this raid had plenty of reason to be scared of Iraqi AAA and SAMs. Especially the AAA fire.

In the 1967 war, Israel lost over 40 aircraft—all to AAA fire, none to SAMs.

They had looked at U.S. Vietnam figures which showed during that ten-year war (1964-1974), 70 percent of aircraft losses were to AAA fire, 15 percent to SAMs and only 6 percent to MIGs. They also had their own experiences which showed similar results in the 1970s including the 1973 Yom Kippur War.

In all the wars since 1960, almost 90 percent of all tactical air losses have been caused by AAA fire. It is estimated 30 percent of all those AAA kills were the direct result of SAM avoidance maneuvering.

One of the key reasons for the success of AAA fire is when SAMs are a threat or are fired at incoming fighters and bombers, the aircraft dodge and weave in the sky to avoid the missiles. They may miss the missiles, but because they are so heavy-laden with bombs, they end up getting in the deadly envelope of the AAA guns.

Almost all losses to AAA guns have been in the 1500- to 4500-foot altitude and within 25 miles of the target— the precise area a plane must be to drop its bombs.

There are three types of AAA fire:

Aimed. Like shooting a flying duck. The gunner tracks the aircraft and predicts where it will be at a certain time, points his gun there, and fires hoping to have the airplane and bullet arrive together at the same point.

Sector. Guns are directed and fired to a specific area which would be the most likely approach an aircraft would use to bomb a target.

Barrage. Hundreds of rounds are fired in a given area to force planes to fly through it en route to the target. This is why the Israelis needed the element of surprise— to keep the Iraqis from having time to set up a barrage of AAA fire that could easily knock down several of their attacking aircraft.

Because of intelligence reports on defenses, it made all the pilots nervous even thinking about the potential air defenses of the Iraqis in the vicinity of the nuclear reactor. But they weren't about to be frightened off.

Getting the planes and bombs to the target and the planes back home again required intricate planning and skillful execution in flying.

The early F-16A single-seat model possessed by the

IAF has a basic weight of 16,500 pounds and a maximum takeoff weight of 35,400 pounds. The Israelis outfitted it with the two MK 84 bombs, chaff and flares, Sidewinder missiles, internal fuel and two 370-gallon wing tanks plus the 300-gallon centerline tank for fuel. When the weight totaled up, the plane weighed 37,947 pounds, or 2,547 pounds too heavy to get off the ground.

For the actual mission, the flight would take off at an elevation 2,500 feet above sea level in 85-degree temperatures—all of which made it even tougher to get airborne.

Usually, a lightly loaded F-16 with centerline tank would leap in the air using less than 1,800 feet of runway at that altitude. But because of all the added weight, it was estimated it would take more than 5,200 feet for the plane to struggle from the runway into the air. Intricate skill had to be used to get the nosewheel tire off the runway at 180 knots or the plane would be badly damaged.

Maximum range cruise speed would be 331 knots and, as the plane got lighter, that speed would get slower. At that speed, the F-100 engine of the F-16 would burn 4,940 pounds of fuel an hour. For the fuel-guzzling afterburner takeoff, low altitude flight to Baghdad, plus acceleration to high speed near the target, afterburner pop-up on target, 9,000 pounds of fuel would be used.

Six thousand pounds of fuel would be left to get home. But there would be less drag without the bombs and wing tanks. Also, high altitude flying on the return flight would require less fuel. Planners estimated there would be 1,000 pounds of extra fuel or 15 minutes of flying time left in the planes' tanks when they landed back in Israel—if all went well. It would be cutting things close, especially if they had to duel in any dogfights with Iraqi MIGs. And after the bombs were dropped, the aggressive spirit of the Israeli fighter pilot in the F-16 if a MIG was in front of him would instinctively be, "Get out of my way, I'm going for him." But at least they could accomplish the bombing mission with hope of return.

General Dynamics had test-flown the F-16 with no bombs or missiles at fuel-saving high altitudes for a maximum 2 hours and 55 minutes. This mission would be 3 hours and 10 minutes, and flown at low altitude with lots of drag from bombs, missiles and full tanks.

The IAF was going to teach the manufacturer just what the F-16 could really do.

In all the world's air forces, there has always been a conflict of youth versus seniority. And nowhere is it more evident than in the IAF.

The younger pilots feel they have the undiminished aggressiveness, sharp reflexes, honed skills and fearless instincts to do the job better than higher-ranking pilots who are getting older.

As U.S. Navy Vietnam ace Randy Cunningham put it in his book, *Fox Two* (that he wrote while a lieutenant), "Why let rank lead, when ability can do it better?" (Of course, Randy is now the commanding officer of Fighter Squadron 126 at Miramar Naval Air Station in San Diego and it's not known if his views on the subject have changed since he has grown in age and rank.)

The same politics of higher rank versus perceived youthful skill played a part in Operation Babylon. Once the F-16 pilots had been ordered to commence low-level navigation training, Dov, Dan and General Ivri started to grade, judge, analyze and select those F-16 pilots who they felt were the best pilots for the mission, the cream of the cream.

Pilot performance in the skies over Lebanon had a lot to do with the selection process.

As in all serious IAF operations, 10 percent of the pilots were to be combat novices. Those selected in addition to Dov and Dan were Samuel, Joseph, Amos, Ben, Gabriel and novice Udi, plus two backup pilots. They ranged in rank from colonel to captain.

Once selected, the group was confirmed by General Ivri and the IAF strike board. But when the squadron commanders and base commander were made privy to the purpose of Operation Babylon, politics entered the selection of the final pilots to fly the mission.

The Wing Commander, Colonel Isaac, insisted on flying the mission. As the senior man of the base where the F-16s were stationed, he had the rank to displace one of the junior men on the attack. It was not a popular decision and created quite a controversy. Isaac was a proven and effective veteran in three previous Israeli wars. His past performance was outstanding and that is why he was a wing commander. There was nothing for him to gain by flying the mission. He was not even proficient in the F-16. But he decided to replace a young captain named Ben who was highly qualified and skilled in the F-16. Ben was furious at senior pilots who had to show their stuff at his expense. He was bumped back as the number one standby pilot for the raid.

Isaac spent extra weeks training in the F-16 to catch up with the other pilots to learn how to handle and feel at ease in the aircraft. He would fly as wingman to Dan, which placed additional training requirements on Dan to help Isaac.

As the senior man, he would get credit for leading the mission, but it was really Lt. Colonel Dov and Dan who did the bulk of the work and planning among the pilots. After all, Isaac still had a full-time job as base commander.

Isaac's attitude was, "We in the Israeli Air Force believe that the commander is always up front; he sets the standards as the leader and commander, so naturally I get more combat missions. I always have to be better and try to do more. It goes with the territory."

Although commitment to the raid was one of the most closely guarded secrets in Israeli military history, the quirks of fate played strange games. Menachem Begin's personal secretary naturally was aware of events to come—and she had her tender concerns. Her son Samuel was one of the top F-16 pilots and she knew he was to be selected to fly the mission long before he did.

Her motherly instincts tugged at her heart-strings with every discussion and preparation for the attack she was privy to while working in the Prime Minister's office. However, she pursued her professional responsibilities with vigor, realizing the security of Israel was at stake, even though it could cost her son his life.

The September 30, 1980, botched Iranian raid sent shivers of fear down the spines of Dov and Dan. They had contempt and disgust for the Iranian failure. The Iranians' poor performance was now to make the Israeli mission just that much more dangerous. Iraq would be on the alert for future attacks and would beef up their AAA and missile defenses.

The Israeli pilots tensely waited for any additional word about the Iranian attack as if their lives hung in the balance—which they did.

Talking about the situation, Dov and Dan figured the losses they would suffer on the raid would be escalated from one or two planes to two or three.

Iraq and some of the world press said the planes in the bungled attack were planes with Iranian markings flown by Israeli pilots. The Israeli pilots and planners quietly reacted with contempt at the naiveté of the press about the complexities of properly carrying out such a mission and the theory that the Israelis would risk their lives based on crude Iranian maintenance, supply, intelligence and reliability.

The planners estimated eight bombs would be needed to hit the target, requiring four planes, so the number of planes to be sent on the mission was doubled as insurance the task would be completed.

As preparations for the attack intensified, Dov and Dan got a cryptic message to fly down to Tel Aviv to meet with Chief of Staff General Rafael Eitan and Air Force Commander David Ivri.

Though the subject wasn't outlined, they suspected it would be Operation Babylon. It's rare for air force lieutenant colonels to be asked to meetings with the top brass.

Arriving at the headquarters, the two pilots were ushered into Eitan's spartan office.

"We've heard enough from the staff about this mission; we want to hear from the pilots. What do you think about the raid? Can it be done?" queried Eitan.

Dan looked the general straight in the eye and without a moment's hesitation, blurted out confidently, "Nothing can stop us from destroying the reactor." With a similar concern for his country's future, safety, and not that of his life, the pilot continued, "After that, what does it matter?"

The bushy-eyebrowed general was impressed with the bluntness and concise answer. He was reassured by such a simple statement of commitment from the men whose lives were on the line.

The mission was on.

To get a first-hand feel, Chief of Staff Rafael Eitan even flew on one of the rehearsal missions.

A Sunday was the selected day for the attack, the assumption being that the European experts would not be working then. It was a goof by Israeli intelligence. The foreign workers took off Friday, the Muslim Sabbath, just like the Iraqi workers. Sunday was a work day, but the time of the attack selected by Dov was so late in the day that most all of the workers had left work.

When Sunday, June 7, was selected for the raid by Prime Minister Begin, several operational problems arose.

How could the 12 planes needed for the strike be outfitted with all the external tanks and bomb racks and how could they be flown to Etzion and staged for the attack without causing any suspicion, especially without flying on Saturday, the Sabbath?

Sunday was a bridge day between the Sabbath and the Monday Shavuot holiday. Not much military activity was expected during a holiday period. There was need to be careful not to focus any interest in air force activities.

Air Force Operations decided the planes were to be flown to Etzion on Friday, June 5. Crews prepared them for the flight. They would be flown down in pairs throughout the day to avoid questions.

Dan and Dov were told on Thursday that they were to leave the following day for Etzion. At home that evening, Dan read stories to his young children as they sat in his lap. After tucking them into bed he lingered in their darkened bedrooms and reflected on the dangers to come and his love for those kids. Those youngsters were his life, and he wasn't sure he'd ever see them again.

Friday morning, Dan told his wife Ruth he was going to the south for several days of exercises. Since his base was located in the north, it was highly unusual for him in peacetime to be assigned to the other end of the country.

"Why the south?" she asked with concern. She felt different this time about his leaving. She didn't know why, but she was scared.

Dan just shrugged, hugged and kissed his children and Ruth goodbye and left for the squadron. He maintained total secrecy for the mission, even with his own family.

Meanwhile, Dov was having other problems. His wife Sarah wanted to know why he couldn't let some of the other squadron members go south for the training exercises. After all, he was the commanding officer and this was a special holiday weekend and she had arranged a large party for some friends.

Just a month earlier he had gone to another training exercise and missed her May 10 birthday. Why did he have to go again? He tried to explain about his responsibilities as a leader and commander, but she wasn't having any of it. She wanted him there that weekend. It wasn't a pleasant parting.

To continue the secrecy of the mission, the planes left Ramat David in radio silence, just in case anyone was listening to radio communications and trying to gather intelligence on air force movements.

The technical representative of General Dynamics assigned to Ramat David to help the Israelis with development problems on the F-16 was nearly fired for

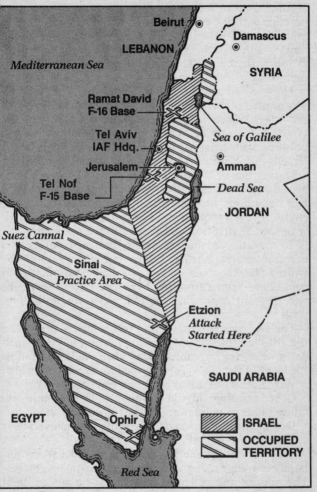

Beirut

LEBANON

Mediterranean Sea

Damascus

SYRIA

Ramat David
F-16 Base

Sea of Galilee

Tel Aviv
IAF Hdq.

Jerusalem

Amman

Tel Nof
F-15 Base

Dead Sea

JORDAN

Suez Cannal

Sinai
Practice Area

Etzion
Attack
Started Here

SAUDI ARABIA

EGYPT

Ophir

ISRAEL

OCCUPIED
TERRITORY

Red Sea

The main locations of military activity involved in Operation Babylon are noted here. Israel is a small country although at the time of the raid the Sinai was part of its territory and contained two key air bases.

not reporting about the raid in advance. But he had become used to seeing the planes come and go during practice with the extra tanks, so he really didn't give it much thought as the planes lifted off for Etzion with the tanks—although this time they had an unusual configuration with the 2,000-pound bomb racks attached to each wing.

The U.S. air attaché at the U.S. Embassy in Tel Aviv was nearly sent packing back to Washington for failure to provide advance intelligence about the raid and the Israeli F-16 training. The hapless attaché just had no advance knowledge or access to any information the Israelis didn't want to share. And it wasn't by accident.

During the 1973 war, the U.S. Air Force attaché had been so talented, sensitive, respected and interested in IAF operations, he was virtually adopted as "one of the guys." He even spoke fluent Hebrew. He spoiled the IAF with special attention and they returned the favor.

To the attaché and his deputy assigned during this event, it was just one more duty station. As a result, the United States lost out on lots of valuable information it could have gained from the IAF. These two Americans were insensitive to what the IAF was trying to accomplish.

The IAF was so upset with their behavior it revoked the attaché's informal permission for him to visit Israeli bases whenever he wanted. They then made him follow the letter of the law to get approval to visit a base, which required plenty of advance notice and paperwork.

Other training throughout the air force continued. Other pilots were unaware of the impending attack.

Dog-fighting practice or air combat maneuvering is continuous in the IAF. And it's dangerous.

On Wednesday, June 3, two Israeli-made KFIR fighter-bombers were mixing it up in mock air-to-air combat. The pilot of one pulled his nose up as he made a tight turn to escape the aggressive tactics of his "enemy." He lost airspeed, rolled over and entered a flat spin. His plane started to gyrate violently.

Yoram, the young pilot, struggled frantically to get his plane back under control. The KFIR twisted around in a corkscrew pattern as it rapidly sank toward the earth. He lost more than a thousand feet of altitude with each 360 degree turn. His fellow pilot, watching in horror as the plane spun, initiated short bursts of conversation on the radio with his out-of-control "adversary."

"Opposite rudder, neutralize the stick," he pleaded with Yoram, his voice muffled as he talked through his oxygen mask.

"I'm, ah, ah . . . , er, trying," came a grunt in reply as the G forces were tossing Yoram around his cockpit.

"Come on, Yoram, come on, get it stopped."

"I can't . . . ah . . . ugh . . . it won't stop . . . er . . . ah . . . ah spinning."

As they passed through 5,000 feet, his wingman pleaded, "Get out, Yoram, get out. You're getting low. Eject, Yoram, eject!"

"Wait, I think . . . I think . . . I . . . ugh . . . can save it."

"Eject, eject now!" came the cry.

Silence was the answer.

There were no more radio calls.

No white billowing parachute.

Twisting in circles the plane hit the desert floor and exploded, and a plume of black smoke drifted skyward from the desert floor like a giant column. The wingman radioed back to his base and reported the crash.

A high-level Operation Babylon planning meeting was interrupted shortly later when Chief of Staff, Maj. Gen. Rafael Eitan, was notified that his son Yoram was killed in a plane crash. He went into immediate mourning.

Meanwhile at Etzion, the planes, pilots and some of the support crews arrived on Friday. The mechanics began to check and recheck the aircraft to be sure all systems worked perfectly. The distinctive white circle with the six-point blue Star of David on the wings and the squadron insignia on the tail were painted over. The planes on this particular mission would be F-16s painted only with a lizard blend of sand, dirt brown and wisps of green with no identifying symbols.

That evening, the pilots went to a movie on the base.

The next day, Saturday, was leisure time. In the afternoon, they went over to the gym for a friendly game of basketball.

Dov's squadron against Dan's.

It started off slow, but as the competitive and aggressive pilots got into the game, it became a real duel with plenty of elbowing, butting and hip-shoving.

They finally had the good sense to end it after Joseph was decked in one rough and tumble scramble under the basket.

Fortunately, no one was seriously injured.

That evening they slept in a large dormitory. But getting to sleep was tough. All the men were nervous about the next day's mission. After lights out, they started telling stories and jokes to ease the tension. And then the men began to grow quiet, lost in their thoughts or trying to get some sleep as they stared at the ceiling or tossed about.

It was a fitful night with little sleep for any of them.

15

The Brief

SUNDAY WAS A quiet day for the pilots. They had a restless night's sleep and lounged around well past the normal 0600 wakeup call. Some coffee, tea, rolls and fresh fruit had been brought to the dorm early.

There wasn't much talk.

Everyone was lost in his own thoughts about the impending dangers. This wasn't the typical combat mission most had faced in the past. There were a lot of unknowns—and it's hard to prepare for unknowns.

Too much time before a dangerous mission makes for a lot of nervousness. And there was a lot of time to think. Normal fighter air combat missions from Israel happen quickly without a lot of forethought.

You're on a combat air patrol, sight MIGs, get ground clearance to attack and are off for the engagement and kill. Entire elapsed time: less than five minutes.

Or you're at war and flying sortie after sortie without time to really think between missions. You're too busy refueling, rearming and itching to get back to the combat zone, like an athlete intent on getting back in the competition.

If you're not flying, you're envious of those who are and are anxious to relieve them in the cockpit when they land, especially if they've scored some kills. The pace is furious.

But this mission was something new for the IAF. Plus the added pressure for absolute success—there'd be no second chance because secrecy is a one-time occasion.

Until 1100 they sipped coffee and tea and nibbled at the fruit and rolls while they again reviewed their flight plans and studied intelligence reports, even though they knew them by heart.

The day's scheduled briefing was the third for the flight crews. The previous two flights had been canceled. But there was a feeling in the air today that this was the real thing.

The pilots sorted maps and flight information neatly and clipped it to their knee-boards, so they could flip through and check for the needed data in sequence as the flight progressed. Their knee-board checklists included all the code words for the flight.

Although they weren't hungry, they had a full early lunch. They would need the energy for the next seven hours. Everyone realized this might be their last meal. And everyone knew some of them would not return.

To lighten the air after the meal, the always optimistic Joseph told Amos, "I'll bet we all make it back."

"Oh yeah, and what kind of stakes do you want to place on that kind of talk?" Amos scoffed.

"The winner buys dinner for the group at that high-class Alhambra restaurant in Tel Aviv."

"You're on—and I hope you win. That's one bet I won't mind paying off," Amos said.

Following lunch, it was off to the briefing room for the noontime meeting. Tight security prevailed, even on the already-secure base. The pilots were surprised to see Chief of Staff Gen. Raphael Eitan when they entered the room. He was unshaven and red-eyed, but his uniform was starched and clean. The death of his son four days previously had been a tragic loss. Traditional Jewish custom was a seven-day mourning period in seclusion with no interruptions, no work or socializing.

Now, here he was. He wanted to be with his men. It

was a sensitive time. They were impressed he was there. If it was that important to him to be at the brief, they recognized all the more the significance of the flight.

Only those directly involved in the mission were at the briefing. It was limited to the eight selected pilots and two standby F-16 pilots, the six F-15 pilots from Squadron 133, the two-man F-15 crew who would orbit high over Saudi Arabia as a communications relay station, Air Force Commander Lt. Gen. David Ivri, plus four intelligence staff briefers including the head of military intelligence, Gen. Aluf Yehoshua Sagi.

The pilots sat in arm-chair desks with pencils in hand ready to write notes on their knee-boards. The brief started with weather reports. It was simple. Skies were clear with some buildup of cumulus clouds along the route over the mountains. Desert heat would make for a bumpy flight down low.

"All you new guys at flying, take an airsick bag," the briefer lamely tried to joke. There was a little forced laughter at the briefer's effort at lighthearted humor. But the atmosphere remained tense and business-like.

Contrails could be expected in the mid-30,000-foot levels and strong jet streams to the east at about 40,000 feet. The intelligence briefer reviewed the fact that Sunday was a holiday and no European workers were expected to be at the site.

"What if they are?" asked Gabriel.

With a stern look and tough, almost bitter voice, General Ivri interrupted to respond, "We didn't ask them to be there. We warned them and the leaders of their countries many times to go home. If they don't want to, they are on the side of terrorists and whatever happens to them is their choice."

General Sagi then refreshed all the pilots' memories with ground photos of the site and the cupola that was their target. He also gave Israeli intelligence a review of expected antiaircraft defenses of SAM 2's, 3's and 6's in the dense protective zone 12 miles out from the city of

Baghdad. He updated intelligence on the emplacements of the ZSU 23-4 radar-guided 23-mm antiaircraft guns as well as 57 mm flack guns and 14.5- to 23-mm cannon optical-aimed AAA guns.

If the surprise attack were discovered, the ground fire aimed at the attacking aircraft could be withering. He cautioned that he felt the effective low-altitude SA 6 ground-to-air antiaircraft missiles would be the most dangerous threat. It was still a heavily fortified target and estimates hadn't gotten any more optimistic since intelligence briefings during training and for the scrubbed flights scheduled previously.

"We've studied and studied and everything we can see and hear about the Saudi AWACS flights flown by the Americans shows their powerful search radar extends out about 350 miles," Sagi went on.

"They only have four of the big aircraft, and we expect only one to be flying while you're in the air.

"Their normal search pattern is toward the Persian Gulf so you should be safe from their detection. Besides, you'll also be out of their normal search ranges. Your route takes you about 300 to 400 miles north of where the AWACS should be.

"We've plotted your course to stay out of Jordanian air space and away from their radars. That's why we're taking the longer route that dog-legs south of Jordan, rather than a straight-line course.

"We think there is a hole—a strip of desert all the way to Baghdad with no radar coverage by anyone. If there is, you should be undetected. But keep your eyeballs peeled and your head on a swivel, just in case.

"We don't have any way to jam their search radars; it would take one of those giant four-jet AWACS type of plane to generate enough power to block all the ground radars to shield your entry. There's just not enough power available in your size aircraft," concluded the general.

This part of the briefing took 30 minutes. At the close,

Major General Yeheshua Saguy, head of Israeli Army Intelligence. (AP/WIDE WORLD PHOTOS)

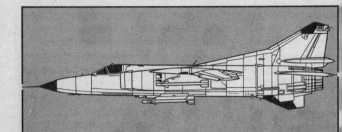

MIG-23MF FLOGGER-E

MIG THREAT

This Russian-built MIG-23 can reach speeds of 850 knots. Although it would be no match for either the F-16 or F-15 in a dogfight, its Apex missiles can take head-on shots at the F-16s.

The Israeli F-15s fanned out to protect the attacking F-16s from this effective interceptor which they anticipated the Iraqis would launch from airfields surrounding the reactor site.

ZSU-23-4 23 mm

THREAT TO THE ISRAELIS

This weapon is a modified tank that is fully tracked, armor plated for protection of the crew, and self-propelled with a turret that can rotate 360 degrees in 4 to 5 seconds to easily track incoming bombers. It has a radar dish in the turret that seeks out and locks on aircraft targets at which the four 23 mm guns open fire.

Each of the guns pumps out 400 rounds per minute which take about 7 seconds to reach the target. The guns are effective up to 10,000 feet. Accuracy of fire greatly diminishes when the aircraft fly at speeds greater than 300 knots. This loss of accuracy was one reason the Israelis flew at such high speeds during the diving attack.

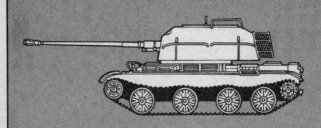

ZSU-57-2 57 mm

THREAT TO THE ISRAELIS

This Twin 57 mm fires about 100 rounds
per minute from each barrel with a maximum effective range between 10,000 and
14,000 feet when visually directed. If radar
directed, they can accurately hit aircraft in
the 15,000 to 20,000 altitudes. When the
shell explodes, lethal shrapnel blasts 30 feet
in all directions, ripping apart any airplane.
This weapon also fires orange and red
tracers that look like flaming beer cans to
the pilot. When the projectile explodes, the
airburst gives a deadly white puff as the
fragments seek to penetrate the skin of an
airplane.

a female intelligence aide, Ophir, tidied up all the intelligence data, wistfully looked at Udi with her big, brown expressive eyes, puckered her lips and blew him a sad kiss as she prepared to leave the room. They had been dating for more than a year. He gave her a cocky smile and a shy, chest-level wave of the hand. It belied his inner feelings of worry and concern over his first combat mission.

Dov now started the mission brief which took an hour and a half in a tension-filled atmosphere. He went step-by-step through the flight reviewing call signs, launch time, take-off procedures, courses, altitudes, radio frequencies and radio silence procedures, code words and procedures in case of INS failure, check-point code words and emergency procedures.

He listed the key frequencies and code words on the blackboard as the pilots rechecked them on their knee-boards.

"On the way in, if you have an engine failure," said Dov, "zoom up about 100 feet to gain altitude before ejection. Your momentum should carry you up to 500 feet for the actual ejection. A search radar makes a sweep every 12 seconds. If there is radar—they'll only catch your blip once and think it is a mistake when it doesn't show up on the next sweep.

"You'll probably get two oscillations in your chute before you hit the ground. Drink some of your emergency water when you get on the ground. It'll help you get over the shock of bailing out. Then gather up your parachute and bury it the best you can so it isn't accidentally spotted," he warned.

"Wait till dark before activating any emergency signals or using your PRC 90. That should give the rest of us time to hit the target and be on the way home. The helos are expecting a nighttime rescue. When you hear them coming, it's okay to light a rescue flare," said Dov.

"We can't afford any chances on discovery or any strange events like a rescue beacon that could cause

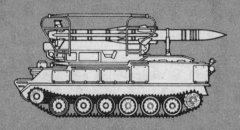

**SA-6 GAINFUL
SURFACE-TO-AIR MISSILE**

SAM THREAT

This SAM 6 missile launcher carries three 1,300-pound missiles which are fired individually or in salvo at the incoming enemy plane. The missiles are guided by the straight flush radar vehicle. Israeli pilots most feared this Russian-built and Iraqi-operated defensive system.

attention to us prior to the attack. This must be a surprise if we are to be successful," Dov emphasized.

"It'll be sweltering hot in daytime, but that desert will be icy cold and windy at night, so get mentally prepared for it.

"The CH 53 rescue helicopters will take off one hour prior to our launch. That will place them halfway to Baghdad while we are dropping our bombs. They will have aerial refueling capability from C-130s. Their call sign is 'Angel.'"

Dov continued, "If you are hit by a missile or AAA fire and can still fly—head west as far as you can before you eject. The choppers will try to pick you up, although they are instructed to keep out of a 25-mile radius of Baghdad and those concentrations of air defenses. No use losing more people to AAA fire.

"So if you're over Baghdad when you eject, just walk west—and fast," he said with a smile.

"Darkness should protect the helos from MIG attack during any rescue. The helo pilots don't know our target and should you be rescued, don't tell them."

Dov said, "All radars will be on standby. Put the DME part of Tacan in standby so it doesn't radiate signals; IFF to standby/receive only. We don't want any RF signals coming from our aircraft.

"I'll break radio silence as we cross the four checkpoints on the way in so headquarters can track our progress.

"At the 38-degree longitude point, it will be 'Charlie,' at the 40-degree point it will be 'Zebra' and at the 42-degree mark it will be 'sand dune yellow.'

"As we cross over the small island in Bahr al Milh Lake, I'll call a final position report. All communications will be in English, so anyone listening might confuse them with international commercial air traffic," he added.

"We'll fly spread formation, just like we've been practicing. It has several advantages. If someone crashes because of fatigue, we don't all crash, and some get to the

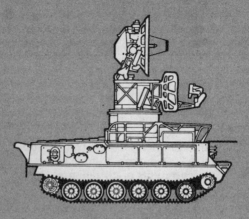

**STRAIGHT FLUSH
RADAR FOR THE SA-6**

SAM THREAT

SAM missiles need radar guidance to hit an airplane. The dangerous SAM 6 system surrounding the Iraqi reactor consisted of this radar which could lock onto the F-16s and guide the telephone-pole-sized SAM 6 up a beam till it hit the attacking plane in an effort to destroy it before the bomber could drop its bombs. This radar has the ability to send numerous missiles simultaneously towards one aircraft.

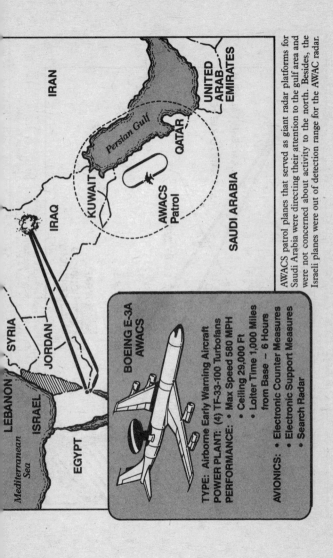

TYPE: Airborne Early Warning Aircraft
POWER PLANT: (4) TF-33-100 Turbofans
PERFORMANCE: • Max Speed 580 MPH
• Ceiling 29,000 Ft
• Loiter Time 1,000 Miles
from Base – 6 Hours

AVIONICS: • Electronic Counter Measures
• Electronic Support Measures
• Search Radar

BOEING E-3A
AWACS

AWACS patrol planes that served as giant radar platforms for Saudi Arabia were directing their attention to the gulf area and were not concerned about activity to the north. Besides, the Israeli planes were out of detection range for the AWAC radar.

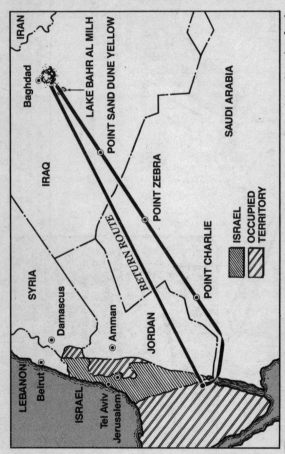

The route to the target 600 miles away in Iraq dog-legged around Jordan after leaving Etzion air base in southern Israel and followed a narrow path designed to avoid any radar detection by Jordan, Saudi Arabia, or Iraq prior to surprise arrival at the nuclear reactor. Return high altitude flight back to Israel was direct and overflew Jordanian air space.

target. It'll make less noise and if we are spotted on the ground it won't seem like as many planes as we are. We'll call ourselves 'Blue Flight.' "

Dov said, "Samuel, you're Blue 2; Joseph, Blue 3; Amos, Blue 4; Dan, Blue 5; Isaac, Blue 6; Gabriel, Blue 7; and Udi, Blue 8.

"The F-15s will be 'Red Flight.' Abraham will be Red 1; Yitshak is Red 2; David, Red 3; Jacob, Red 4; and Moshe and Levi, Reds 5 and 6.

"It'll be line abreast. In our first group, Amos, you'll be on the far right, then Joseph, then me; and Samuel, you'll be on the far left.

"We'll fly about 2,000 feet apart—just so you can see the whites of each other's helmets.

"If something happens to me before the lake, Dan, you take the lead and finish the mission. Forget about me. Joseph, move your flight behind Dan's flight. If I am lost after the lake, Joseph, you lead the flight in. It's too late to change positions.

"Dan, your group should follow about 12,000 feet or two miles behind us. Don't overrun us," continued Dov.

"And keep this spacing until the lake, then drop back to four miles. It will be important when we arrive at the target to be at four miles. We don't want you too close so that the concussion of our bombs blows you out of the sky. Fragments from the explosion of the big MK 84 are advertised to go as high as 3,000 feet in the air.

"Also, if some enemy fighter should jump our group on the way there, you will protect us by firing a Sidewinder up his tail.

"The F-15s, Abraham, should fly in pairs outside our formation. Abraham, you and Yitshak on our left, David and Jacob on our right about 4,000 feet out, and Moshe and Levi should bring up the rear in the center about 4,000 feet back.

"Your F-15s must protect us from any MIGs.

"All you F-16 drivers love dog-fights, but under no circumstances are you to drop your bombs to engage any

MIGs. That's the F-15s' job. Your job is to make it to the target and bomb the reactor.

"After that, you can fight your way home, but remember, we'll just have enough fuel to get home. There will be no tankers or air-to-air refueling. So let's not try to get engaged. Let's destroy the reactor and get safely home," said Dov.

"We'll feed fuel from the wing tanks first. They should last for the first 55 minutes of the flight. When they're empty, jettison them. So far, those external wing fuel tanks have never been jettisoned from an F-16 with 2,000-pound bombs right alongside them. Our test pilots and engineers have calculated they should separate without any problems. Let's hope so.

"In the F-4, sometimes they would tumble over the top of the wings. The F-16 has hinges that should avoid that problem.

"The radar formula says if we keep our altitude below 100 feet, the maximum distance any ground search radar can pick us up is 12 miles away. If we can pull that off, it will be a complete surprise. Staying so low, we should be lost in the ground return clutter that looks like snow on the radar scope.

"It'll be close to sunset and we'll be coming out of the sun for the attack. That should make it hard for them to visually see us and easier and safer. Our arrival time should put us there about five or ten minutes before dark.

"The Bahr al Milh Lake will be our final checkpoint and IP [Initial Point] as we line up our final course for the target.

"It should take us 100 minutes from takeoff till we release our bombs. When we reach the lake, arm your bombs and select all switches for the attack," said Dov.

"Shortly after we leave the lake, Iraqi search radar should pick us up and the SAM sites will be alerted.

"At this point, pay close attention to your radar warning receivers—they'll tell you which missiles are being fired, and the number in the circle will tell you which is your worst threat.

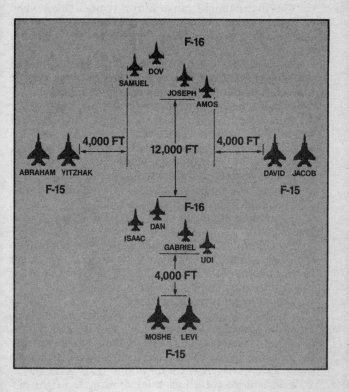

The spread out formation flown by the F-16s and F-15s on the way to Iraq was for safety and defensive reasons. If jumped by enemy interceptors, the planes had enough maneuvering room to beat off the attack. The F-15 outriggers were positioned to protect the F-16 bombers from any Iraqi MIGs. At ground-level high-speed navigation, the slightest error could cause a plane to crash.

"About this point, MIGs should be scrambled from the bases to the northwest of Baghdad and the ones to the southeast as well.

"The F-16s should move into a tight 'welded wing' bombing formation in a slight echelon position as we continue for the target so you're all ready for the bomb drop when we get there.

"Be sure you're spaced out behind the pair in front of you so we will reach the target thirty seconds apart," Dov told the pilots. "We can't afford any mistakes.

"Check your SAM radar jammers at this point.

"Samuel and I will be first in. Gabriel, you and Udi will bring up the rear. As we cross over the lake, the F-15s should climb to form the combat air patrol and protect us from the MIGs. Abraham, be sure your guys form a barrier between us and the MIG airfields.

"By now, the Iraqis' radar will know we're there. The F-15s should turn on their search radar to hunt for the MIGs as they climb up. Everyone still keep radio silence."

Dov continued, "When we cross the Bahr al Milh, all the F-16s should turn on their VTR cameras. We've got to have photos of the damage to bring back with us so the intelligence guys can know what happened.

"Dan, you got something to say?"

"Yes, all we've got are the ground pictures and plans. Here's a drawing I've made. Let's call it 'a view of a wingman.' It shows what the target should look like from the air as we line up to drop our bombs—you can see the dome and the Tigris River off to the right," said Dan.

"Dan, you've got a knack for drawing the right pictures. Thanks.

"All right," said Dov, "remember now, as you dive in to drop your bombs after the pop-up maneuver, put the bomb fall line on the target and the computer does the rest. When the death dot inside the pipper is on the reactor dome, release your bombs.

"Remember—keep your wings level. There can't be

any slipping, sliding or skidding or the bombs will miss the target.

"The hard part will be to do all this while the SAMs are coming at you along with all the AAA fire exploding in your face as you're diving, and the threat of MIGs.

"We've got to destroy the target, no matter what the cost. All bombs are to be aimed on the cupola, the dome. That is the main part of the reactor. There is no secondary target.

"This will be tough for you, Dan, 'cause you're so used to always being up high in dog-fights rather than down low pounding the sand with bombs like some of the rest of us."

Laughter.

"Just remember," added Dov, "stay close together, it makes for a smaller target. And don't follow too closely. We don't want the bombs in front of you to knock you out of the sky if they go off early.

"But don't drag too far behind either. Each extra second the Iraqis have before we are out of there gives them more time to shoot and that means more flack and missiles you guys in the rear will have to dodge. So keep it tight. Exactly 30 seconds apart.

"Gabriel and Udi will probably get the worst of it. Dan, it's important you get lined up and spaced exactly right as we leave the lake.

"We'll pick up speed to 480 knots for the approach. That's eight miles a minute, so a 30-second separation will be four miles. You can get your spacing on the radar.

"You all know this, but remember, we'll try to fly at speeds that are easy to convert to minutes, like 360 knots equals six miles a minute, 420 knots is seven miles a minute or 480 knots is eight miles a minute.

"When you drop your bombs, get G on the aircraft immediately and break out of plane so you can defeat any missiles or aimed AAA. We'll be coming in from the south, and egressing west toward home to save fuel. Do at least a 4G turn on the climbing turn up to defeat the

This is the actual drawing referred to in the book as the "View from the Wingman" drawn by Dan. It shows the lead two F-16s pressing the bombing attack on the reactor site.

missiles fired at you. It'll also put us climbing into the sun or what's left of it, which should make it hard on the eyes of their gunners.

"You've got your flares and chaff, if you need them.

"If you get indications of any SAMs on your radar warning receivers, don't be afraid to use the stuff. As you know, the flares work like high-powered flashbulbs and explode behind your aircraft brighter and hotter than the engine exhaust. They should confuse and attract any infrared guided missiles. They'll explode harmlessly on the flare and not you.

"The chaff—thousands of strips of shredded tinfoil—should reflect a better target for radar-guided missiles to home in on than our F-16s.

"Once clear of the immediate target area, go to burner and let's get the hell out of there. But don't use it too long. We need to save fuel.

"Right after we're off target, join up and check in with me on the radio with your number.

"As we climb up, turn on your IFF [Identification Friend or Foe] system. We want to identify ourselves to the F-15s on their radar so they don't accidentally try to shoot us down thinking we are MIGs.

"Once everyone has checked in, I'll call back to headquarters and let them know how many of us made it.

"That call code will be 'Flash.' If we have any losses, I'll add that number after the word.

"They'll have a Boeing 707 communications command post airborne over Israel that will be a communications link to relay our messages all the way back to base. The radios in our planes won't go that far. This will be the first time in history IDF headquarters will monitor the progress of a raid and be able to talk to us in action.

"Moses, you'll be in the airborne command post F-15 orbiting high over Saudi Arabia. You'll serve as a standby communications and command link. It's my understanding if we have any questions or decisions different from the plan, we call you on the radio to get instant orders to make changes in the plan. That will give us the flexibility to get the mission done," said Dov.

"We'll proceed direct to Etzion and overfly Jordan on the way home. Once again we'll fly best economy cruise speed. The INS will figure it out for us. My calculations show it will be 90 minutes on the return leg.

"We'll fly a loose formation on the way home. That way in case we're jumped by MIGs, we can protect each other. Watch your fuel, we'll be low by the time we reach home.

"There'll be fighters orbiting over Israel at our ETA over Jordan, just to provide us with extra air cover in case the Jordanians scramble to attack us on the way home. We don't think they will, but keep your eyes open. We'll call for help on channel 7 if we're attacked.

"Our GCI [ground-controlled intercept radars] will also be monitoring for any Jordanian air activity.

"It should be near dark when we arrive back in Israel.

"Any questions? Yes, Dan?"

"Do we have any idea how many SAM 6's are deployed in the area of the reactor?" he asked.

"General Sagi?"

"There is a brigade of SAM 6 missiles at the site. As you know, a brigade has five batteries and each battery has 12 missiles," said Sagi. "That means they have 60 missiles to try to knock the eight of you out of the sky—or just about eight missiles per aircraft. And remember," Sagi added, "the SAM 6 is smokeless, impossible to see with the human eye, and will be coming at your plane nearly two and a half times the speed of sound. Pay close attention to your warning devices. It'll give you the clues you need to dodge those killers.

"Our agents in the plant work force don't have much freedom to nose around. That's all they've been able to observe," concluded Sagi.

"It isn't the SAM 6's I'm worried about, but the MIGs," interjected Dov.

"I've already gotten 15 of them; they're no problem," responded Dan.

Dov pressed on. "What intelligence do we have on the MIG alert scrambles?"

"From what we can find out," responded General Sagi, "they are doing a poor job of stopping the Iranian attacks and at least half of the time don't even try to intercept them. Of course the Iranians are doing a lousy job of bombing, so maybe the Iraqis don't figure they are much of a threat.

"Dov has done a good job of picking the timing so you'll bomb with daylight and it'll get dark within minutes of that—which should make it hard for the MIGs to follow and find you.

"I agree with Dov, the real threat will be the SAM 6's," General Sagi continued. "If this raid isn't a surprise and they get enough time to warm up their SAM radars and fire the missiles, you've got real problems. It was a deadly aircraft killer in the Yom Kippur War. It has a 175-pound high explosive warhead sitting on that telephone pole-sized missile. It can kill an airplane as low as 100 feet up to 35,000 feet in the sky and they launch them in salvos of three. A very dangerous animal," the general concluded.

"Any other questions?" asked Dov. "OK, good. The F-16s are all parked at the north end of the north-south runway. It's our longest runway, and we'll need most of it to get airborne. They are too overloaded to taxi out from the hangars.

"Abraham, you and your men will taxi out from the underground hangers in the F-15s for a 1455 [2:55 P.M.] takeoff.

"We'll man our aircraft at 1400. At 1430, we start engines and check out all our systems.

"We have four standby F-16s out there. Ezer, you and Ben will man your standby aircraft and if any of the rest of the flight has a problem with their planes, you will automatically move up and replace them.

"Two of the standby planes will be empty with crew standing ready. Those are for either Dan or me if we have a problem with our planes.

"It'll all be by hand signals. We keep radio silence. There will be no talk with the tower. The airfield is all ours for this afternoon.

"While we test our systems with engines running, we burn internal fuel. Just before takeoff, there'll be four fuel trucks there to hot refuel us with engines running so we have our tanks topped with every drop they can hold.

"Launch for the F-16s is 1500. If there are no other questions . . . yes, General Eitan?"

General Eitan stood up, walked to the front of the room.

A hush fell over the briefing room. Everyone was aware they had lost a fellow pilot and he had lost a son just days ago. He began to speak.

"This is an important mission," he emphasized, "and a dangerous mission. I worry for your safety. If something happens, I want you to know that we'll do all we can to rescue you.

"Don't try to be some special kind of hero in the face of torture," said General Eitan. "Tell what you have to. We want you back with sane minds. We understand what you'll be going through.

"Your government and the people of this country are appreciative of your efforts and sacrifice."

Every eye was riveted on the general.

"Your willingness to risk your lives, so we might live, will never be forgotten by Israel.

"This is no ordinary mission," he continued. "Never before has the Israeli Air Force flown an attack to such a distant point—and for such an urgent need.

"Our history as a nation and as a people is at stake.

"You've all read the Bible. You know the history of our people. You know how God brought Moses and the Jewish people out of Egypt. You know the battles Joshua fought to gain entry to the promised land. You know about the just rule of King David and the wisdom of Solomon. You know about the dispersion to Babylon.

"We've kept our identity as a people. And now, nearly 2,000 years later, we are reunited as a nation.

"Our people have overcome the agony of the Holocaust. We've gone through a modern-day Exodus. We've survived wars in 1948, 1956, 1967, the War of Attrition in 1970 and the 1973 Yom Kippur War. And now we are faced with the greatest threat in the long history of Israel—annihilation and destruction of our country with atomic bombs by a madman terrorist who cares nothing for human life. We must not allow him to achieve the ability to build the bomb that could destroy us.

"That's what this mission this afternoon is all about. Protecting our country. The future of Israel rests on your skill and ability to destroy that nuclear reactor. You must be successful—or we as a people are doomed.

"This is a pivotal point in the history of Israel!"

He concluded by saying, "If we are to live by the sword, let us see that it's kept strong in hand rather than at our throat."

The pilots were spellbound by General Eitan's brief but eloquent five-minute speech.

The general, realizing the impact his remarks had on the young pilots, tried to break the tension by reaching into his pocket and pulling out a branch of dates—the most prevalent fruit of Iraq.

"Here, have some of these, you'll have to get used to them where you're going if you get shot down."

Laughter broke the silence of the hushed audience as the pilots got up from their seats to share in eating the dates with General Eitan.

A waiting photographer was brought into the briefing room.

"Let's get a group picture," said General Ivri, "before you all go."

Amos and Isaac refused. They were superstitious and feared bad luck on the raid if they had their photos taken prior to the completion of the mission.

The rest grouped together for the photos. There was no other historical record of the briefing for Operation Babylon. At this point, everyone was worried about success rather than history.

"All right, time to go," said Dov.

"God be with you," beckoned General Eitan as the men filed out of the briefing room to man their aircraft.

It was back to the dorm to suit up for the mission. There was more than the usual concern about the fit of the flight suits, G suits, survival gear, torso harness, and other survival gear.

A slightly uncomfortable flight suit was no problem during a normal 40-minute flight. But the discomfort of being tightly strapped in for two and half hours could gnaw painfully at some pressure point on the skin and be distracting—just when total concentration was needed.

Each pilot strapped two PRC 90 radios to his torso harness. The PRC 90 is a compact two-way radio about the size of two cigarette packs which allows a shot-down pilot to communicate with his airborne fellow pilots. It also sends out a homing signal to aid rescue aircraft so they can pinpoint the downed airman. No one ever carries two radios. This mission was an exception since there was no walking back from it and no one was taking any chances in case one of the radios failed.

Once they were all suited up, they stacked up their shaving kits and clothes. They would be flown back to home base Ramat David by transport to be reclaimed by them or their next-of-kin after the mission.

16

Operaton Babylon

". . . His Excellency is over Israel,
and His strength is in the clouds."
Psalms 68:34

AFTER THE BRIEFING and suiting up, all pilots clambered
into four waiting vans. Weighted down by all their gear
and flight helmets, the men plunked down into their
seats. They drove to the maintenance operations center
where each man signed for his aircraft and checked
maintenance discrepancies—just like a normal training
flight.

Anxiety was in the air. The room was full of aircraft
crew chiefs and maintenance workers milling around
trying to look busy, but sneaking glances at the pilots. All
knew something special was about to happen—but no
one knew what. They felt like privileged witnesses—
realizing they would be as close as anyone could get to
the action.

The F-15 pilots headed to their camouflaged underground hangars not far from the end of the runway. Their
F-15s had been armed with four Israeli-made heat-
seeking Shafrir air-to-air missiles and four radar-guided
Sparrow missiles—enough missiles among them to blast
48 enemy aircraft from the sky—not counting the 512
rounds of 20-mm cannon fire that could rip a MIG apart
with just a short burst as they fired at 6,000-rounds-a-

minute. The world's finest air force wasn't about to take any chances of losing an F-16 due to enemy MIGs.

There was a shortage at the time in the IAF of all-aspect Sidewinders (AIM 9L) or heat-seeking missiles that detect not just the tailpipe exhaust of a MIG, but the heat caused by the friction as it flies through the air.

These better missiles were mounted on the F-16s. With their superior radar detection fire control system, the F-15s would get the Israeli-made Shafrir missiles.

The big conformal fuel tanks had been bolted onto the side of the engines and were topped off with jet fuel.

The F-16 pilots were driven to their armed and waiting aircraft at the end of the runway. It was a silent ride— each man mulling over what he had to do and anxious to get started.

The quiet time was painful. Nerves grew tense.

"Give me some action to keep me busy and get my mind off waiting," thought Dov.

It was a hot afternoon as the Negev Desert sun baked the runway. As Dov looked down to the end of the runway where the planes were parked, he could see waves of heat radiating upwards, forming a mirage on sizzling concrete.

Finally they got to the standby alert aircraft sheds. Four F-16s were parked in the square, open-ended Quonset huts.

The huts gave the alert air crews some shelter from the sun and concealed some of the mission from satellites or high-flying spy planes.

Snoopy high-tech intelligence-gathering devices really didn't matter now, because even if U.S. or Soviet intelligence organizations learned of the concentration of aircraft, there wasn't time to figure out their purpose or how to stop them. The desert base of Etzion was too remote and secure for any viewing from roads or towns.

The other eight F-16s were lined up nearby.

Because of the overloaded condition of the F-16s, no one wanted to taxi around sharp corners. It could put too much pressure on the wheels and landing gears which could cause them to collapse. It was also questionable how well the brakes would work with that heavy a load.

The ten pilots walked around their planes for a complete preflight check for hydraulic leaks, fuel leaks, bomb attachment, missile placement, tire pressure, damage to aircraft skin—anything that could jeopardize the success of the flight. Their crew chiefs had already carefully checked the planes and made any necessary adjustments prior to the pilots' arrival.

But the pilot bears ultimate responsibility for the aircraft—and his own neck.

Special ordnance crews had attached the powerful 2,000-pound MK 84 bombs and safety-wired the fuses to avoid accidental detonation. Deadly Sidewinder 9L air-to-air missiles had been attached to each wingtip. The F-16s' centerline 300-gallon tanks were full, as well as both 370-gallon wing tanks.

The small fighter looked heavily burdened—quite unlike the way it appears in the sleek, glossy General Dynamics' publicity photos. But it was a deadly load, the real reason this plane was built.

Helped by their crew chiefs, the pilots climbed up steel-frame ladders into hot cockpits. First chore was to get comfortable. Then each pilot attached the parachute risers from the ejection seat to his torso harness just above each shoulder. That way, if he ejected, the emergency parachute stuffed inside the back of his seat would be attached to him when he separated from his seat after both left the aircraft in an emergency situation.

Next, they plugged in their G-suit fittings to blow up the balloon-like bladders. Then they attached to themselves a survival kit strapped to the seat of the torso harness, and finally they hooked themselves to the seat belts. There wasn't much room for movement.

The crew chiefs then handed the pilots their helmets. Radio leads and oxygen masks were plugged in, helmets were donned and fire protection gloves were pulled on. Amos had the glove tip on his left index finger clipped out so he could watch the color of the quick under his fingernail to detect if his oxygen system worked properly. If his fingernail turned purple, he would know hypoxia was setting in and could take corrective action before he lost consciousness from lack of oxygen.

Knee-boards with maps and vital mission information were strapped to both thighs which made for easy writing by the right-handed pilots.

The crew chief double-checked the pilot's parachute fittings, and ensured all safety pins were removed so the ejection seat was armed and ready. To get out of the plane in a hurry, all the pilot had to do was to pull an ejection handle attached to the seat and brace his head against the head rest on the back of the seat. A rocket would shoot him hundreds of feet into the air and he was guaranteed a safe parachute ride—even if the plane was standing still.

Then the crew chief either slapped the pilot on the shoulder or shook his hand with a long look that said, "I don't know what you're doing, but good luck," and then scampered down the ladder and removed it from the side of the plane.

Each pilot started going over his checklist of dozens of items and checks of switches prior to starting his engine. At precisely 1430, Dov lifted his right hand and waved his index finger in a circle indicating to his crew chief he was going to start the powerful F-100 Pratt & Whitney engine. The other nine pilots followed suit.

Soon all ten engines were whining so loudly that it was impossible to talk anywhere on the tarmac.

Once the engines were started, the pilots closed the bubble canopies and turned the planes' environmental control systems (air conditioning) to full in an effort to keep cool as they sat under the blistering sun. There were no sunshades. It was like being in a greenhouse.

Each pilot started checking, double-checking, and triple-checking all the plane's systems. He would enter the flight course coordinates into the inertial navigation system (INS), check, then double-check, to be sure of accuracy. There would be no room for errors.

This was the loneliest time. Tension mounted. Nothing to do but check, and recheck the systems, and wait.

About ten minutes into the checks, Dan's heart sank. His entire electronic system failed, including his navigation system and missile-jamming equipment. He furiously pushed and pulled knobs and switches remotely associated with the system, hoping something simple was wrong. Despite the air conditioning going at full blast, rivers of sweat poured from his forehead and body.

This plane had been his exclusively for the last six months. He'd lived with it more than he lived with his wife. Every practice flight for the mission had been made in this plane. It had never let him down before.

Now, just 20 minutes from takeoff on this critical mission, systems that were absolutely vital to the success of the flight were out of order.

He had no choice. He had to switch airplanes. It was like losing a close friend.

Was it a good or bad omen?

He wouldn't be in his own airplane. It had failed him. Sure they were both F-16s, but each plane has it own little characteristics and idiosyncrasies. Now he'd be in a new and different plane which wouldn't have the same angles of sighting for the guns and bomb drop indications.

All kinds of gloomy thoughts raced through his mind.

But he had no choice. Dan raised the canopy and was blasted by the desert heat as he frantically waved for his crew chief. He pulled back on the throttle to shut down the engine. As the ladder was placed alongside the plane, Dan unstrapped and scrambled down from the cockpit. He gave a quick thumbs down to the crew chief, but couldn't verbally explain the problem above the nearby screaming jet noise of the other nine planes. It didn't matter. Time was too critical now.

He made a mad dash for his backup F-16 and climbed into the cockpit, got strapped in and started his engine and continued his preflight checks. Everything in this plane checked out okay.

But it still gnawed at him. Did switching airplanes mean more trouble later?

Seven minutes to takeoff and the fuel trucks started the "hot refueling" to top off the tanks of the eight scheduled aircraft plus the two backups.

During the warmup period, they had burned 300 pounds of valuable fuel.

Joseph's plane was having problems. His refueling system wasn't working. The fuel wouldn't transfer from the truck into his aircraft. What to do?

"I've spent the last six months preparing for this ride, I'm not canceling now. I'll just be careful the way I handle the throttle," thought Joseph.

Udi's plane was having problems too. "I'm going to risk it," he thought.

The other six pilots' planes refueled with no problems.

The end of the runway was now alive with noisy activity. The F-15s had taxied up from the underground hangars and were going through runway preflight checks. They were thundering down the runway in pairs, then leaping into the sky. They would loiter to the south, waiting for the F-16s to join them.

When flight leaders Dov and Dan looked over to check their respective groups, all pilots gave a "thumbs up"— ready to go.

Neither Joseph nor Udi told anyone they would be leaving 400 pounds—or eight minutes of flying time— short on fuel. (Note—400 pounds represented 300 pounds burned while waiting and 100 pounds burned while refueling.)

It was already close as to whether the F-16 could fly to Baghdad and back without an engine flameout due to fuel starvation. Now Joseph and Udi would be pushing their luck even further.

It was 1457. Dov nodded his head forward, pointed his hand and forefinger straight ahead and taxied over to the threshold end of the runway. The others followed.

The ground crews, wearing noise-dampening earmuffs,

went through a series of quick checks of the aircraft and control movements. They hand-signaled the pilots that all systems were in a "go" condition.

Then the squadron ordnance crew carefully pulled the safety pins from the bomb fuses and ejector charges in the pylons and held their hands in the air displaying the long, red ribbon bands on the pin-ends to each pilot. The bombs were now armed and ready to explode when released from the aircraft at the end of each designated arming delay.

While going through the arming procedures, Dan could hear himself breathe as the microphone in his oxygen mask transmitted to his helmet earphone. He'd never consciously listened to his breathing before. Now it was obviously labored, heavy and fast as he sucked in and exhaled his oxygen from his mask. It was a reminder to him how taut his nerves were. "Let's get going," he thought.

Dov was tense as he pushed his throttle forward to 100-percent power and then into afterburner. He heard the engine wind up and he started down the long runway. The afterburner plume shot out the powerful exhaust. Slowly Dov gained airspeed.

The mission had started.

Slightly behind and to the right, Samuel was glued to him in a formation takeoff that placed him acute of the wing line, almost looking in and reading Dov's knee-board maps and cards.

Dov's plane passed the 1,000-foot runway marker. Airspeed 90 knots. He continued to accelerate. Two thousand feet. His airspeed now read 124 knots. Normally, he'd have been airborne by now. The plane gradually picked up speed. Three thousand feet.

"This is slow," he thought. But he remembered an old phrase from his Hill AFB training: "The faster you go, the faster you go faster."

It took 15 seconds to reach 100 knots.

In the next five seconds, he'd reach 150 knots. It took 180 knots to get airborne. Four thousand feet; 145 knots.

Panic flashed through his mind. After all this, to wind up a pile of burning rubble at the end of the runway, because we were too overloaded.

He thought to himself, "I'd rather have gone at max weight and taken my chances on the way back of ejecting and being rescued than to have the embarrassment of never getting off the ground."

He hadn't envisioned himself piloting the world's fastest tricycle. He carefully nursed the nosewheel up, just lightly, not a jerk to "unstick" it, but just enough to let it ride free, keeping the weight on the main mounts.

At 5,000 feet, he twisted his right hand to put an ever-so-slight back pressure on the control handle. The speed slowed one or two knots, but then resumed.

The F-16 struggled into the air at the 5,200-foot marker. One hundred and eighty knots. Samuel was right with him.

The test pilots and engineers were right. The F-16 would fly with such overloading.

"Boy, if we get through this mission, this will be the best advertising General Dynamics and Pratt & Whitney ever had. Now, let's get to Baghdad," thought Dan.

Ezer and Ben in the standby aircraft saw their chances to be part of IAF history fade as the flight of F-16s followed each other down the long runway. As the last pair of F-16s left the runway, they shut down their engines and slowly unstrapped and climbed out of their planes. They would be called to stand by another 15 minutes, but for all intents and purposes, they would not be a part of this history-making mission.

General Eitan, after assurances from Ivri and a special code word from the airborne leader, called Prime Minister Begin on a secure line as soon as the planes had departed, and notified him the mission had begun.

Immediately, Begin had his secretary contact all Cabinet members and request them to come to his home at 4 P.M. No reason was given for the sudden invitation. Each member thought he was going to have an exclusive session with the prime minister on this Shavuot holiday eve. Their minds revved up about subjects they wanted to cover as well.

As they drove up, the ministers' cars were whisked away and they were ushered into the living room of his Jerusalem home in the fashionable Rehavya district. As they started to congregate in Begin's home, the Cabinet members were puzzled as the place filled up with their colleagues and they tried to figure out what had happened to their precious exclusive meeting with the prime minister. Many were disappointed, for the moment.

After General Eitan's call, Begin stepped out of his private office and went down the hall to his study where his ministers were sipping tea and making small talk while waiting for him.

"Gentlemen, eight of our planes are now on their way to bomb their target in Iraq. I hope our boys will be able to complete their mission successfully and return to base."

The Cabinet was stunned.

One minister attempted to correct what he thought was a mistake: "You mean the missiles in Syria?"

"No, the Iraqi nuclear reactor at Al Tuwaitha outside of Baghdad," replied Begin.

Then he sought advice. "What should Israel do if the attack fails?"

The astonished leadership of Israel were momentarily speechless.

Dov headed south and started a slow, curving left turn to the east so all the planes could execute a "running rendezvous" and get together after takeoff. To avoid Jordanian air space, they would go south about 25 miles before crossing the Gulf of Aqaba at an isolated spot over the Sinai.

Dov was skimming over the desert floor at 100 feet and about 2,500 feet above sea level. Already the drag and low altitude could be felt on the fuel flow.

To follow the contour of the land, he and his flight had

to climb to get over the craggy mountains on the edge of the 3,500-foot gulf and then back down to cross the eight-mile-wide gulf that separated the Sinai from Saudi Arabia.

The flight was now in a spread-out line abreast formation with pairs boxed. The F-15s were in visual sight. Radio silence still prevailed.

They were now going to penetrate Saudi air space south of Haql, an abandoned airfield, and the village of Al Humaydan.

The red mountains in the area had some peaks 5,600 feet high, but the attacking planes wove through the valleys. It took less fuel than climbing and descending and it made any radar detection virtually impossible.

The mountainous terrain was a stretch of 40 miles and took seven minutes to transverse. Then it was the flat, scorching-hot wasteland desert of Saudi Arabia. They hugged the desert floor.

Forty miles later they crossed a small paved desert road and abandoned railroad track which connected Tabuk with the southernmost point in Jordan. Previous intelligence operations and continuous monitoring showed no radar coverage of this area below 7,000 feet that was dependable. As they crossed the road, each pilot looked for any vehicular traffic.

A long silver tanker fuel truck was dead ahead.

"Ah, nuts," thought Dov. Then he reassured himself, "At least he won't have a two-way radio way out here that could alert anyone."

They had to stay far enough north of the big Saudi base in Tabuk. It had surveillance radars and occasionally fighters were deployed there. Then it was mile after barren mile of nothing but sand and occasional sagebrush.

Dov was continually monitoring his navigation aids and checking his wingman. He also checked his onboard computer to keep track of his best cruise speed for his aircraft weight as fuel was burned.

He was the leader and the same information would

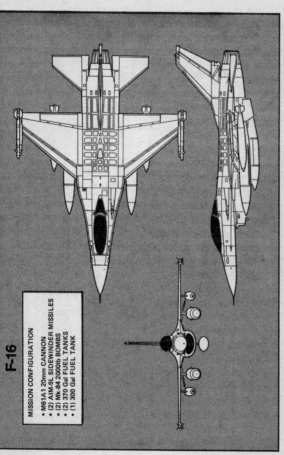

F-16

MISSION CONFIGURATION

- M61A1 20mm CANNON
- (2) AIM-9L SIDEWINDER MISSILES
- (2) Mk-84 2000lb BOMBS
- (2) 370 Gal FUEL TANKS
- (1) 300 Gal FUEL TANK

A fully armed and fueled F-16 as it looked when it left Erzion air base for the raid. Notice Sidewinder missiles on wingtips, MK 84 2,000-pound iron bombs, and the two dropable wing fuel tanks on each wing. The centerline fuel tank stayed with the aircraft throughout the mission. Flares and chaff used to aid in defeat of Iraqi missiles were loaded near the tail of the F-16.

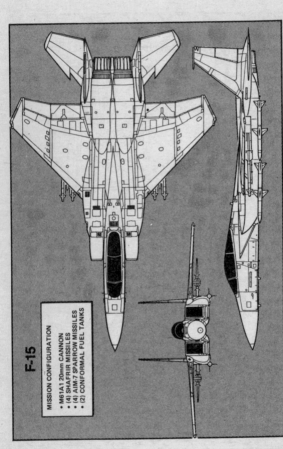

F-15

MISSION CONFIGURATION
- M61A1 20mm CANNON
- (4) SHAFRIR MISSILES
- (4) AIM-7 SPARROW MISSILES
- (2) CONFORMAL FUEL TANKS

The F-15 as it was armed to fly Operation Babylon. Each of the six protective fighters was armed with four Shafrir (Israeli made) heat-seeking air-to-air missiles and four Sparrow radar-guided missiles. That was enough firepower to knock 48 Iraqi jets from the skies. In addition they had a 20-mm cannon Gatlin gun in the nose of the plane that fires 512 rounds of ammunition on board the F-15 at the deadly rate of 6,000 rounds-per-minute. The conformal or fast-pack fuel tanks are attached alongside each engine and nearly double the range of the F-15.

apply to the rest of his flight. Dov was attempting to be as smooth as possible, giving the formation lead time and a percent or two in power during turns to assure minimal power oscillations through the formation. It took real concentration.

Best cruise speed early in the flight was 360 knots, but as the planes used fuel and became lighter, that speed decreased.

The heat from the sunbaked sand radiating upwards bounced the planes around and took intense concentration to control as they skimmed over the desert floor.

Dan was also checking his gauges. After changing planes, he was extra alert and sensitive, worrying about something going wrong. As he sped along, his mind flashed back and he saw the faces of his daughter and son at home playing. He couldn't figure it out. He felt so close to them—and had such a longing to be with them—yet here he was on his way to his possible death in a foreign land.

They reached the 38th longitude. The simple word "Charlie" broke radio silence. Not enough for anyone to track and get a bearing on, but enough to give the IAF Headquarters a progress report on the flight.

General Ivri, in the "hot seat" command post, passed the call to Eitan, who informed Begin.

It was picked up by the orbiting RC 707 over Mitspe Ramon and relayed down to the southern command center and IAF headquarters simultaneously. There were a lot of people on the ground sweating out this raid.

Dan's mind continued to wander as he subconsciously flew the airplane just above the desert sand, howling along at tree-top level—if there had been any trees in the desert. They were flying so low the shadows on the late afternoon sun made the sagebush look like giant trees.

His mind flashed back to his pilot-training days and how the majority of his carefully selected class flunked out of the complex and demanding course.

His ears still rang as he remembered his acrobatic

instructor angrily yelling during one check ride: "Almost perfect isn't good enough. Take me back to the base and you go back up alone and practice and practice and practice. Do it over and over again till you get it perfect. That's the only way you'll get your wings in this air force!"

He recalled a second lecture from his instructor: "There are four types of students in flight training: Those who think slow and decide wrong. Those who think slow and decide right. Those who think fast and decide wrong. Those who think fast and decide right.

"It's the last group we want in pilot training."

There was no friendship between students and instructors. It was all business—a screening process—and the future of Israel was at stake.

The fuel-warning gauge jolted Dan back to reality. The wing tanks were running dry. Everyone in the flight was starting to get the same indication. Dov got concerned.

Time to jettison the 245-pound, 370-gallon tanks on each wing to get rid of the aerodynamic drag. Those tanks had never been released from the F-16 with 2,000-pound bombs attached right next to them. Would they separate clean—or would they tumble into the bombs possibly causing the airplane to go out of control? There weren't enough tanks to test out what would happen before the flight.

Dov reached for the release button that would activate the release pin and separate the tanks from the plane.

"Maybe it would be better to keep the tanks on the aircraft," he thought, "and be sure nothing could possibly happen to affect the mission."

The others were watching to see what he did. Dov thought to himself, "I've got to release them. The airplane would be clumsy to handle for an accurate bomb drop, to avoid antiaircraft fire and missiles, and then to attempt a dog-fight.

"Besides, the drag will burn up so much fuel we'll never get back to our base."

He pushed the switch and rolled the plane to look out

the left side to see the tanks float away and then tumble as they headed for the desert floor. Then he lost sight of them.

There was no banging or jolt to the F-16, but speed did increase at the same throttle setting as the plane got aerodynamically cleaner.

Dov relaxed and checked his navigation INS system. He was right on course—and on schedule.

Then he saw Samuel and Joseph release their tanks and gave them a reassuring "thumbs up" as he confirmed their tanks had separated okay. So far, so good.

Dan had released his tanks, checked out his flight and system instruments and then found his mind wandering again. He was concerned about the SA 6 missile threat. For the last ten years, all his flying experience had been in the two-seat F-4 Phantom. If he was shot down, he'd have had company as a POW. Having someone there with him would make the ordeal easier to tolerate, he thought.

"Now, if I'm shot down in the single-seat F-16, I'm all alone. Could I stand the isolation?" he wondered.

"What does it matter—being Jewish I'd never get out alive. They'd probably hang me on a wooden cross," he thought.

He looked out his canopy to the left and saw some jagged rocky outcrops in the desert. To the right were sand dunes. Sakakah airfield ought to be to the north.

Dan tuned in the Al Jouf vortac navigational aid. It indicated a bearing to his 11 o'clock.

"Zebra" cracked briefly in his radio headset. He checked his INS and thought, "Dov's got us right on course."

Now Dov turned to his left about 30 degrees and took up a heading for Bahr al Milh Lake—still sand-blasting over isolated desert areas.

Udi, streaking across the desert on his first combat mission, was jittery. But he was thinking how to collect his memories. Then he hit on a plan. The HUD TV camera had a 30-minute video tape. The most the camera would be turned on from Bahr al Milh Lake till they were clear of the target would be 15 minutes. So he spent part of the other 15 minutes of the tape on the way to the target vividly recording the event.

On part of his video film he captured pictures of holiday groups on the shore of the lake cheerfully waving to the screaming fighter-bombers thinking they were their own.

"What irony," he thought. "Here are Iraqis intent on destroying our country when we've never done them any harm. Now we're going to annihilate their nuclear capability before they can use it against us—and they're waving to us." He rolled the plane slightly to the right and gave the sunbathers the finger in response to their waves.

Fuel burn was 75 pounds a minute.

Dov picked up speed to 390 knots as the planes grew lighter. Then he radioed "sand-dune yellow," the final checkpoint before they arrived at the lake.

So far it was an uneventful flight, but one that had captured everyone's total attention and concentration. Now all the pilots scanned the skies even more earnestly. They were approaching defended territory.

The radar detection device alerted.

"Oh no," he groaned. "We're being tracked by search radar from here to the target—15 minutes. Everyone in the country will know we're coming by the time we get there."

He visualized greater losses than he or Dan ever figured.

"I just hope we can hit the target before they destroy us," he thought.

Each man reviewed his entry checklist in preparation for crossing the lake on the way to the target. Then the lake came into view. It was larger than expected.

Dov quickly searched for the main island in the center to update his INS. He couldn't find it. Panic. His stomach knitted. Was this the wrong lake? Had he navigated incorrectly? Where had he led his flight? At six and a half miles a minute, he didn't have a lot of time to figure it out.

He was right on time. It was 1725 local time. They were due on the target at 1735.

All roads checked with his maps. There was a small city off to the right with a tower—that should be Al Mardh. Off to the left was a small town—that should be Ar Rahhaliyah.

Then it hit him. The lake was swollen due to the rains and flooding. The small island was under water and the waypoint cross on the HUD was resting on shallow muddy-blue water. He checked his INS; it was right on, anyway. No need to update it.

He momentarily relaxed. Being right where he was supposed to be and right on time was a confidence builder.

Then he changed course slightly to the right—for Al Tuwaitha and the Osirak nuclear reactor.

Sixty miles to go.

Things were going to get real busy now.

He twisted and wiggled in his seat to get his butt as far back in the ejection seat as possible and his back aligned properly. His movement got the circulation flowing in his legs, but it also got him positioned if he was hit by AAA fire or a SAM and needed to eject. He didn't want to injure his neck from the rocket forces by sitting improperly in his seat as they both shot out of a destroyed aircraft. No use arriving on the ground via a parachute as a cripple. It would be tough enough just being a POW.

He swiveled his head around to check the formation line-up. His squadronmates were right where they belonged. Everyone was lined up just right.

Dov now started a final mental review process for the attack. Was he going to be early or late over the target? It was critical he drop his bombs exactly on time so he didn't foul up Dan's interval and timing.

He switched on his radar and selected the 40-mile range scale. He intently searched the 20- to 30-mile range sector looking for little green squares that would indicate enemy MIGs.

He cross-checked visually out the clear cockpit canopy.

Nothing in sight. So far so good.

Simultaneously he was making one last check of his aircraft systems. Fuel? More than half gone because of this fuel-guzzling low-level flight, but right on flight plan because there would be enough to return home since that part of the journey would be at fuel-sipping high altitude. Engine temperatures and RPM: normal. No electrical problems. Everything was under control.

Now to get his flare and chaff systems set for the bombing run. He was depending upon the chaff to act as a decoy for any radar-guided SAM 6 missiles fired at him. When released from the airplane, the fluttering chaff would rain down toward the ground as a large pattern on radar scopes that hopefully would act as a decoy to attract the SAM 6's fired at him and cause them to explode harmlessly behind him, leaving him free to close in and drop his bombs.

Dov took his left hand off the throttle and reached across his chest in a cumbersome effort to grasp the aircraft control handle on the right side of the plane. That left his right hand free to reach back behind him and feel for the chaff and flare switches.

"Damn," he thought, "why couldn't they have designed this part of the plane better so I don't have to fly in such an awkward position at virtually ground level. One slight twitch of my uncoordinated left hand on the sensitive control stick and I could nose the plane into the ground and become nothing but a streak of shredded metal on the desert floor. It sure would have been a lot easier if they had placed these switches on the left-hand side of the cockpit."

He quickly selected a combination program that would eject 20 bundles of chaff, two every second, during the ten seconds of the pop-up maneuver when he'd be most vulnerable over the target.

Then he programmed the remaining ten bundles to eject from the tail of his F-16 for protection as he left the target.

As he looked up from the cockpit, his heart nearly stopped beating.

Straight ahead he saw them. Metal towers stretched out in a line across the desert, right across his path. He couldn't see the wires but he instinctively knew they were high power lines. They hadn't been on any of the preflight briefing charts. What a surprise. Dov didn't have a choice.

He instantly broke radio silence. "Climb, climb. High tension wires. High tension wires," he warned his fellow attackers.

They all barely missed entangling themselves in the wires that could have meant a premature end to the mission.

"Wow, was that close," he thought. "Now back to the pre-attack check list."

Next he called up his stores control panel on his instrument console above his left knee. It was a digital video-screen type display that lit up with green words and numbers. It showed he had the thumb-operated pickle button on his control stick selected to fire his Sidewinder missiles. This was in case he was intercepted during his journey across the desert to Baghdad.

His left hand gripped the throttle. He took his thumb and moved a three-way switch so the pickle button would drop the bombs instead of firing his defensive missiles.

He'd switch back to missiles as soon as he dropped his bombs and pulled up off the target. He'd need those heat-seeking Sidewinders to protect himself if any MIGs penetrated the F-15 protective cover.

He next checked for arming delay information. This gave him a visual display of the minimum altitude the bombs had to fall from the airplane so the fuses would arm. It indicated a 4.8-second delay from the time they left the F-16 till they could explode. That meant the bombs had to be released so they would fall at least 2,500 feet before piercing the reactor dome. Otherwise they would be duds.

This was a safety precaution with the bomb fuses to protect him from bombs being dropped too low and exploding with high-flying shrapnel that could knock him or those following him from the sky.

He next checked the data on his bombs to ensure both were still attached to the plane (although it was easy to tell they were by the way the aircraft flew), and that they would both drop together when he pressed the bomb release button. He didn't want to make a second pass.

No more time to worry about missiles, MIGs, engine problems or anything else. Just keep the formation together and prepare to bomb.

He looked to the right. Samuel had tucked his F-16 right in close—just as planned. To his rear he could see Joseph and Amos.

He increased speed to 600 knots. The ground was a blur.

He was looking far ahead of where they were and at the same time he watched his HUD. All eyes were now out of the cockpit.

The F-15s on the left went into min-afterburner to zoom up to 20,000 feet and form a barrier between the bomb-laden F-16s and Al Taqaddum and Habbaniya MIG airfields about 35 miles to the north.

They turned their pulse doppler search radar from "stand-by" to "on." With no ground clutter problems or low altitude mainbeam spillage, they could easily spot any MIGs as they would take off. It would be easier to shoot them down when they first got airborne and just out of range of the airfield's protective SAMs.

The F-15s on the right touched burner and shot up to 25,000 feet, peeling off to the right to form a barrier between the F-16s and the giant air base Ubaydah Bin al Jarrah, 80 miles to the south along the Tigris River.

Both MIG interceptor groups stayed out of the high SAM threat area of Baghdad.

The flight of bombers pressed on. They crossed the famed and ancient Euphrates River.

The follow-up pair of F-15s in the rear pulled back on their sticks and in 15 seconds were at 20,000 feet, forming an umbrella over the F-16s to protect them from any MIGs that could get airborne from the three major airfields in Baghdad proper—Resheed, Muthenna and the International Airport.

The INS and the radar now indicated the target 18 miles ahead. Dov could see the buildings and the shiny white dome. They were alongside the Tigris River.

The seconds ticked by.

Four miles from the target. Time to pull up. Dov went to full afterburner and added slight back pressure to the sensitive control handle. He rocketed up to 7,000 feet in four seconds—right out of the sun as planned.

Then he smoothly turned hard left 90 degrees pulling 5.0 Gs, lowered the nose of the F-16 down below the horizon, rolled wings level, engine out of afterburner and dove right down the "chute" for the dome of the nuclear plant.

He focused his total attention on that dome and on his bomb pipper, watching the target as the pipper tracked closer and closer to the planned release point. Dov was in a 38-degree steep dive hurtling for the ground about as fast as a bullet.

He checked his radar warning receiver out of the corner of his eye. No indications of SAMs in the RWR. The RWR was silent. Was it working? Could that really be true? No SAMs?

He cautiously allowed himself to think optimistically for a brief moment, "Maybe we really did surprise them."

He pressed the attack.

Five thousand five hundred feet, 5,000 feet, 4,500 feet. He was screaming for the ground.

Absolute concentration.

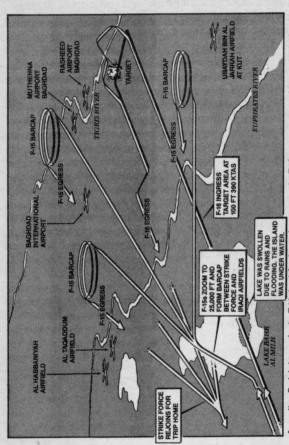

AL HABBANIYAH AIRFIELD

AL TAQADDUM AIRFIELD

BAGHDAD INTERNATIONAL AIRPORT

F-15 BARCAP

F-15 BARCAP

F-15 EGRESS

F-15 EGRESS

MUTHENNA AIRPORT BAGHDAD

RASHEED AIRPORT BAGHDAD

TIGRIS RIVER

F-15 EGRESS

F-16 EGRESS

TARGET

F-15 BARCAP

UBAYDAH BIN AL JARRAH AIRFIELD AT KUT

EUPHRATES RIVER

F-15 EGRESS

F-16 INGRESS TARGET AREA AT 100 FT 390 KTAS

F-15s ZOOM TO 25,000 FT AND FORM BARCAP BETWEEN STRIKE FORCE AND IRAQI AIRFIELDS

LAKE WAS SWOLLEN DUE TO RAINS AND FLOODING. THE ISLAND WAS UNDER WATER.

LAKE BAHR AL MILH

STRIKE FORCE REJOINS FOR TRIP HOME

Immediate Baghdad area. As the F-16s head for the nuclear reactor, the F-15s zoom up to provide a protective barrier against Iraqi MIGs that could be launched to destroy the incoming bombers from the airfields in the Baghdad area. Lake Al Milh and the small island in the center were the final navigation fixes as the F-16s head for the target with bombs armed.

Years of training were now culminating in this one precise moment, to hit a target less than 60 feet wide.

Four thousand feet. Release time in altitude, but Dov thought he'd push down lower just to be sure he hit the dome exactly right.

Samuel was right alongside him in a tight formation to make as small an AAA target as possible and had released his bombs before his leader—precisely at the programmed 4,000 feet.

He started his pull up.

Dov reminded himself not to get target fixation and fly so close to the ground that at this high speed there wouldn't be any altitude left to pull out of the dive.

His thumb rested on the bomb release button on the top of his control stick.

His attention was riveted on the symbology in the HUD. The bomb fall line was tracking right on the reactor dome.

Thirty-nine hundred feet, 3,800 feet, 3,700 feet, 3,600 feet. The altimeter was unwinding so rapidly it looked like a clock in fast motion.

Now the death dot of his bombsight system was in the center of the nuclear dome.

Thirty-five hundred feet. Dov pressed his thumb on the round red bomb release button and pickled off his two MK 84 2,000-pound bombs. He pulled up.

Immediately he selected his fire control radar to be ready to spot and fire his Sidewinders or guns at any MIGs he expected to attack him.

He hit afterburner again and simultaneously pulled his stick hard to the left and climbed out.

He looked over his shoulder while pulling 4 Gs.

His G-suit bladders filled with air. The balloon-like bladders pressed against his thighs, calves and stomach to keep his blood from leaving his head as his 165-pound body now weighed 660 pounds.

He saw the bombs hit and pierce the dome.

"Bullseye, one reactor," Dov thought.

It was the first time in history conventional weapons of

one country had successfully destroyed another country's nuclear weapon capability.

The aircraft shook. Dov couldn't see behind and under himself. Had he been hit by a SAM or AAA fire? He didn't know, but he knew something had happened. He and Samuel joined up on the climb towards the sun. They raced for altitude and out of range of the dangerous SAMs.

Dov turned on his IFF so his own F-15s could spot him on their radar and wouldn't shoot him down thinking he was an attacking MIG.

Next, Joseph and Amos popped up and rolled in for their bombing run on the dome.

It had been partially collapsed and they could see the jagged hole left by Dov's and Samuel's bombs.

Joseph thought, "Dov and Samuel have been right on—now it's up to me to finish the job."

He bore in. A few grey-white fluffs started appearing in the sky. They weren't clouds.

"They're shooting at us," realized Amos. "Never mind, look at the pipper and get those bombs into the dome. Wings level, that's it. Hold it. Now!"

A SAM missile fizzled as it left a corkscrew white smoke trail under them.

Four thousand feet and they released simultaneously.

Dan and Isaac then pulled down after reaching their 5,000-foot pull-down altitude to start their bomb run.

Their timing and interval were precise. Dan had done a perfect job of navigating and closing the gap to exactly 30 seconds behind Joseph and Amos.

They watched the bombs ahead of them explode and shatter the dome.

Dan thought to himself, "There's not much dust. What's wrong—are they hitting it right?" Then he realized, "They're not bombing desert sand and watching lots of dust kicked up by bombs exploding in the loose sand like we practiced—all the dust is being contained in the building."

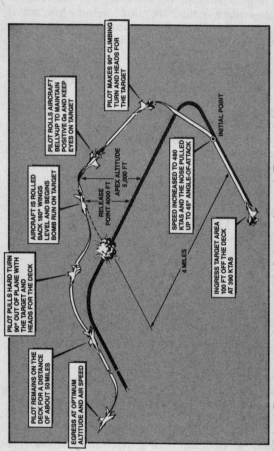

PILOT MAKES 90° CLIMBING TURN AND HEADS FOR THE TARGET

INITIAL POINT

PILOT ROLLS AIRCRAFT BELLY-UP TO MAINTAIN POSITIVE Gs AND KEEP EYES ON TARGET

APEX ALTITUDE 5,000 FT

RELEASE POINT 4000 FT

AIRCRAFT IS ROLLED BACK 180°, WINGS LEVEL AND BEGINS BOMB RUN ON TARGET

SPEED INCREASED TO 480 KTAS AND THE NOSE PULLED UP TO 45° ANGLE-OF-ATTACK

PILOT PULLS HARD TURN 90° OUT OF PLANE WITH THE TARGET AND HEADS FOR THE DECK

4 MILES

INGRESS TARGET AREA 100 FT OFF THE DECK AT 390 KTAS

PILOT REMAINS ON THE DECK FOR A DISTANCE OF ABOUT 50 MILES

EGRESS AT OPTIMUM ALTITUDE AND AIR SPEED

The Israeli F-16 pattern as the planes entered the final stages of the attack. They came in low and then popped up to gain altitude to sight the target and press the attack. After dropping their bombs, the fighter-bombers made an abrupt turn to the left to avoid any SAM missiles fired at them, hugged the ground briefly, and then rocketed to the safety of high altitude.

Isaac had one eye on his pipper—and the other looking for MIGs. He was worried about being jumped while trying to drop his bombs. Isaac also realized his lack of experience in the F-16 wasn't helping him any at this moment. They pressed on toward the target.

Dan drove the two of them down below 4,000 feet, down, down to 3,400 feet before they released.

The area in front of them was dotted with black and grey-white puffs. It wasn't accurate, but the AAA fire was thick and menacing.

Dan had always been the high-flying air-to-air fighter pilot. This low flying was scary enough, but now he was seeing the thickest antiaircraft barrage of his life.

Their planes buffeted as they pulled out.

"What happened," thought Dan. "No time to worry now. Turn left hard and pull up. Gotta get out of here.

"If we get back, we'll look at the HUD video tape and see what happened," he thought.

Gabriel and Udi got the best and worst of it on their pass: the worst AAA fire and the best view of the demolished target as the slightly delayed fused bombs exploded.

None of the ZSU-23-4 radar-aimed AAA guns got warmed up enough to track the F-16 targets. The surprised gunners just tried to operate the AAA guns manually. They put up a lot of flack, but with no accuracy.

SAMs were fired. SAM warnings even showed up on the F-16 alert systems. But no hits.

The surprise of the raid was total.

In two minutes over Baghdad, Israeli warplanes in their surgical strike had reduced Iraq's technological centerpiece to rubble.

Concern over fallout from possibly hitting any radioactive substance on the site proved unnecessary. The attack was done with such pinpoint accuracy that only the dome was hit. The uranium, less than 200 feet away in a bunker, was left intact.

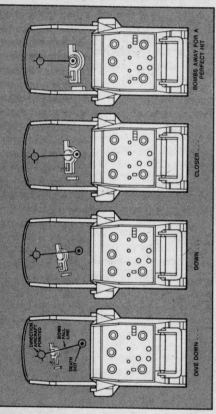

DIVE DOWN . . .   DOWN . . .   CLOSER . . .   BOMBS AWAY FOR A PERFECT HIT

DIRECTION
AIRCRAFT
POINTED

BOMB
FALL
LINE

DEATH
DOT

THE PILOT'S VIEW

The final three to five seconds of the Israeli attack were spent by the pilot intently watching his HUD and lining up the pipper to accurately drop his bombs as he dove toward the reactor. Airspeed at this point was 480 knots.

The Israeli pilots were watching the bombsite with total concentration as they prepared to pickle off their 2,000-pound bombs. Their goal was to get the target lined up on the bomb fall line. The pilot then maneuvered the plane during the bombing dive so the dome of the nuclear reactor stayed on the line. When it appeared in the center of the pipper with the "death dot" in the middle of the dome, the pilot dropped his bombs.

When done properly, the bombs are guaranteed to hit the target due to the excellent F-16 bomb sighting system. While doing all this, the pilot must hold the plane steady with no twists, turns, or jinking to avoid intense anti-aircraft fire aimed at him. He must be oblivious of the bursting AAA surrounding his plane and the surface-to-air (SAM) missiles being launched to intercept him – if he is to hit his target.

The dome of the Osirak plant looked like a giant broken egg shell.

Later, Pentagon spokesman Henry Catto was to say satellite photos showed extensive damage to the Iraqi installation with every bomb scoring a direct hit.

"There was not one crater around the place. Every bomb went where it was supposed to go." Catto expressed admiration for the "technical precision with which Israel carried out its raid," but added, "we strongly condemn the act."

A French worker, Jacques Rimbaud, said two days later that he had watched the raid while sitting on the terrace of a cafe not far from the plant. His comments were interesting in view of the facts.

"Four planes took part in the raid. Two of them made a pass over the plant to check defenses, then the other two followed, dropping four bombs," he said. "All four planes then made another pass, probably to take photographs, before flying off."

He called the bombing accuracy "stupefying."

"When I reached the site, the precision of the bombing astonished me . . . it seemed to me the bombs fell to within one meter of their target," he said.

"As they flew over the last time, the Stalin Organs [multiple rocket launchers] opened up for 15 minutes. There were tracer bullets and antiaircraft missiles fired too."

French electrician Jean François Masciola, another witness to the raid, said the site was surrounded by military defenses and antiaircraft weapons, but they were apparently caught unaware by the attack.

Unfortunately, Damen Chaussepied, a 25-year-old Frenchman, picked that Sunday evening to go to the plant to work. He was the one person killed in the raid.

* * *

The target was 60 feet wide. The 16 bombs were to land within 40 feet of each other and render the reactor useless. One bomb was slightly to the side and destroyed the neutron guide chamber. And one dud bomb failed to detonate after it landed in the center of the reactor.

There was some speculation that the bomb which didn't go off had a delayed action fuse to cause casualties. The Israelis had no desire to destroy lives. All bombs were intended to explode and destroy the reactor. The chances are it was dropped from such a low altitude, the fuse did not have a chance to arm the bomb.

The explosions of the bombs were heard all over Baghdad, but most Iraqis didn't learn what happened until the next day.

A line of barrage balloons designed to ensnare low-flying aircraft floated serenely over the city of Baghdad. But they were too far north of the reactor facility to affect the attack.

Even foreign diplomats stationed in the Iraqi capital were not informed of the raid. About an hour after the attack, the Italian ambassador held a party for the local Iraqi diplomatic community on the lawn of his residence to celebrate Italy's National Day. A special treat for the guests was a fireworks display of red tracers arching through the dark night sky and bright bursts of flack.

But the Israelis were long gone.

However, some Western diplomats said they heard the thud of the Israeli bombs, even before the air raid sirens started wailing and the antiaircraft guns started clattering.

Climbing out, the F-16s rendezvoused as quickly as possible—all in radio silence. Dov was alarmed. He was sure something was wrong with his plane. Through hand signals he motioned for Samuel to get close and check the plane over. Samuel could find no problems.

Like a mother hen, Dov was now trying to collect his chicks. He knew Samuel was okay. Joseph had radioed

"Blue 3"; and Amos, "Blue 4." It seemed like forever, but shortly Dan and Isaac called in "Blue 5" and "Blue 6." Then Gabriel, "Blue 7." Then silence.

"Where's Udi?" Dov thought. "Seven of us have made it and Udi had to get the worst of the AAA and SAMs. Where is he? Did he make it?" Dov's heart sank. The pit of his stomach knotted up. He twisted around in the cockpit frantically looking out the canopy on both sides of his plane for the combat novice.

"Damn, the youngest, the most inexperienced, and we give him the worst position—last—where is he?"

Dov put his finger on the throttle radio switch. Finally, he couldn't stand it any longer. He broke radio silence. "Blue 8, Blue 8, where are you?"

Udi was startled to hear his call sign on the radio. Then it dawned on him, he was supposed to have checked in. "Blue 8 okay . . . joining up," he radioed. It was to be the only slip-up that deviated from the brief.

A relieved Dov led the group up in altitude.

He radioed "Flash" to the orbiting 707 which relayed the word to IAF Operational Headquarters that all the planes survived the attack and were heading home.

The higher the altitude, the better the fuel economy.

They were racing the setting sun all the way back to Israel.

As he climbed higher, Dov checked his own on-board computer for head winds. The weather forecasters were right—38,000 feet had the least head winds, but when the hot jet exhaust would blow out into the cold moist high-altitude air, it left white streak-like powdery chalk lines indicating right where the airplanes were.

The contrails were easy to spot by the enemy.

He climbed to 40,000 feet, no contrails—but 125-knot head winds.

Dov had a choice—either risk detection with the telltale white streaks in the sky or head winds that would slow them down so much the F-16s would surely run out of fuel before they reached Israel.

He chose 38,000 feet for the return trip.

The F-15s, with plenty of extra fuel, climbed to 41,000 feet and kept a close eye on their F-16 charges.

The F-16 exhausts continued to streak contrails like strands of white yarn more than six miles behind each aircraft—eight telltale streaks. All dead giveaways for intercepts by enemy aircraft.

There was jubilation in the inner sanctuary of the IAF Operations Headquarters when they heard the code word that the mission was successful—and with no losses.

They notified Generals Eitan and Ivri at Etzion.

General Eitan called Prime Minister Begin.

"Mr. Prime Minister, the mission was accomplished without losses. The planes are returning to base."

"Let me know when they get back," Begin responded.

Begin jubilantly shared the news with his Cabinet.

There was relief and as the ministers waited for word that all planes had safely returned to their base, they discussed how to handle releasing news of the raid to the press and public.

Dan and Isaac were worried about their aircraft. The buffeting and thumping that each took while over the target had both of them scared that something was wrong. But neither could find anything wrong with the other's aircraft as they flew around each other looking for some telltale sign of trouble.

When the F-15s heard "Flash," they picked up their charges on radar and closed the formation—still arranged to provide air cover and mother the F-16s all the way home.

There was no air activity from any MIG base. They were dumbfounded that there had been no attempted MIG interceptions.

On the way back, Dov was so relieved he was singing out loud in his cockpit as he watched his instruments for any sign of malfunction. He still suspected a problem.

They had accomplished their mission—and with no losses. The pressure was off. Too good to be true!

"Let's just hope the Jordanians don't challenge us as we go directly home over their territory," he thought.

There were no other scheduled radio transmissions the rest of the flight. But Joseph couldn't contain himself. "Alhambra," he radioed. The pilots were reminded that Amos was on the hook for one big dinner in Tel Aviv.

Amos and Joseph were flying so close that Amos could give Joseph a vigorous "thumbs up" between cockpits—only too happy to pick up the tab in realization that he and all his fellow pilots had survived the attack.

For the first time in the history of the IAF the headquarters had gotten on the radio directly to combat pilots while they were on a mission. "Good job, now make a safe landing," came the message.

Dov tried to think of some clever response. But he was so excited he couldn't think of anything original or historical to say, so he just radioed back, "Roger."

He computed his fuel load. Their conservation on the way to the target had paid off. They had some extra fuel, so he picked up the speed home.

The 90 minutes it took to get back to Israel seemed to drag on. Joseph and Udi were extra attentive to their fuel flow after failing to top off their tanks before starting the mission. But they were convinced they would make it back without problems.

Finally, Elat came into sight, then Etzion. Dov had kept the flight high to save fuel. Now the fighter pilots just had to pull back on the power and dive to lose altitude fast—like ducks coming in for a landing.

King Hussein of Jordan, an accomplished pilot himself, was vacationing at Aqaba, the Jordanian city adjacent to Elat at the top of the Red Sea, and could have been one of the first to see or hear the returning raiders as they were letting down.

No one on the base knew what their mission had been, but most knew something unusual had taken place.

The base and the other air bases in Israel had been

placed on alert as soon as the attacking aircraft left. Standby fighters and pilots had replaced the departing F-16s at the end of the runway at Etzion, all in anticipation of attack by some unexpected enemy.

After the takeoff, the crew chiefs surmised it would be a long flight from the heavy fuel load. They played dominoes while they waited. After two and a half hours, they quit and just quietly stood by the maintenance buildings waiting—waiting to spot some small, dark spots in the eastern sky.

When the first dots showed up, the crewmen eagerly counted the number of returning aircraft as they landed in the last shadows of daylight.

It was an anxious ten minutes while the planes gradually showed up. Eight F-16s and six F-15s. All had returned home. The relieved ground crewmen were ecstatic. None of them had lost their planes or pilots.

General Eitan called Prime Minister Begin for the last time. "All planes have returned safely," was his message.

"Baruch hashem," Begin replied in Hebrew.

"Blessed be God."

17

Debrief

THE F-16s LANDED at Ezion and the F-15s flew directly back to their base at Tel Nof. The attack pilots were directed to taxi to underground hangars all still in radio silence.

They parked under a flood of lights not seen above ground and climbed out of their planes in sweat-soaked flight suits. Each shared mechanical concerns with the crew chiefs.

Dov, Dan and Isaac personally checked over their planes, carefully looking for flack or bullet holes.

They could find none, but ordered the ground crews to go over every inch of their fighters while they debriefed with Generals Eitan and Ivri.

All the pilots were ecstatic—they had suffered no losses.

The pilot who had missed the dome and destroyed the adjacent building was feeling low and disgusted with himself.

On the way to the debrief, the others tried to comfort him.

"We did enough damage to the main building," consoled Dov.

"Don't worry about it, you got in some good damage," Dan told him sympathetically. "We took more aircraft than we needed to get the job done and that was one of the reasons. One of your bombs hit the main target—forget about the other."

The F-15 airborne command general in the standby communications plane was airborne for the entire mission. Everything went so smoothly he was never needed or contacted.

The pilots were all tired and relaxed as they met with the generals and intelligence staff. As soon as they could be transported to the debrief room from the underground hangars they were served soft drinks and coffee. Everyone had questions. But now that they were safely back to Israel, the pilots' mood was more casual. The edge of excitement and tension had worn off.

"It was just as we briefed," said Dov matter-of-factly. "No problems or anything. I couldn't believe it—no SAMs, no MIGs—we caught them totally asleep."

The generals had dozens of questions, but the pilots had nothing to add of any consequence. It was later to be described as a relatively boring debrief. Finally, the maintenance chief brought in the gun camera VTRs. Seven of the eight cameras had worked. It was revealing and they all watched in quiet intense concentration as they were played on a TV monitor. The pilots were able to see the sequence of the bombing, the accuracy of their bombs, and increasing flack as each film was shown. A blow-up of one of the frames clearly showed the dome crumbling and crashing into the cooling pool. The film from Gabriel's and Udi's cameras was the best. They even recorded the earth shaking as the bombs ahead of them exploded.

The pilots took a last gulp of their coffee and sodas and went back to their aircraft. The ground crews had found nothing wrong with any of the planes.

The only logical answer to concerns on Dov's, Dan's and Isaac's aircraft was that shock waves had shaken their planes because they dove too low to release the bombs, and were jolted by the explosions and enormous concussion.

Tired but happy, they mounted their refueled birds for the short hop back to Ramat David. Dan was so elated over the mission success, he took his flight of four up north at supersonic speeds and rattled windows the length of Israel. Holiday mood residents didn't give it much thought, but it gave Dan an emotional way of releasing his tension over the raid.

He knew there would be no punishment by superiors on this day for the brief infraction of air force rules against supersonic flight over populated areas.

"After what we've accomplished today, no one can touch us," he thought.

Once all the F-16 pilots arrived at Ramat David from the Sinai base, they were herded into a small twin-engine propeller transport for the 30-minute nighttime flight down to Tel Aviv for debriefing by all the headquarters brass.

The finest pilots in all Israel who had accomplished the most dangerous and vital mission in IAF history were now bunched into one small plane.

After all the meticulous care and planning of the raid, no one seemed to give much thought to what would happen if that plane carrying all eight F-16 pilots crashed and the reservoir of talent were all lost at the same moment. And all the information they gained from the flight to Baghdad would be lost. The flight to Tel Aviv turned out to be uneventful.

Just outside the city, they entered a small guarded auditorium deep inside the secure compound of the IAF headquarters. They were greeted with a standing ovation by their peers—the two dozen staff people who monitored the preparation and the flight.

There was so much excitement and shouting of questions it was hard to keep order. Dov just kept saying, "Everything went as planned; everyone worked like a machine. There's nothing more to say."

It became obvious through the questions that the political leaders were more afraid about possible failure of the raid than the pilots were.

The general in charge of IAF operations exclaimed they had been puzzling over the code word "Alhambra." They had gone over and over their briefing papers and the operation plans while waiting and couldn't find the word. They worried and puzzled about its significance. "What did it mean?"

Dov laughed, "You tell 'em, Joseph!"

And Joseph shared with the attentive crowd about his bet with Amos. There was a cheer when he completed the story and requests from many to join in on the celebration.

The pilots were so tired, relieved and matter-of-fact about the flight debrief, the audience didn't feel satisfied with the answers to their questions. They chewed over and had detailed questions about each small action during the flight. Of course, most had worked over half a year on this project and wanted to savor all the details. But there just weren't any exciting stories to share. All contingencies had been planned for and were solved before the raid took place.

The pilots were sworn to secrecy and flown back to Ramat David to return home to their families as if it had just been another two and half days at the office.

Resting around the house on the Monday of the Shavuot holiday, Dan and his wife Ruth heard the 3:30 P.M. announcement on the radio. The bulletin was a surprise to him after all the secrecy stressed to him. He didn't say a word.

Ruth turned to her husband, pride in her heart and tears welling in her eyes, went over to him and gave him a long, tearful embrace. She turned her head and whispered in his ear, "Now I understand why you've worked so hard the last six months."

Miscellaneous Postflight Facts

The F-16s used in the raid were scheduled to fly the next day. All were manned by pilots, but not a single one of them got airborne. Each plane had some minor malfunction that kept it grounded.

When he arrived at his squadron commander's office, Dov shook his head in amazement. "It's some kind of miracle, the success of that raid must have been God's will. Imagine, all the planes worked perfectly when we needed them."

The U.S. Air Force commands took a long time to believe the raid was done without air-to-air refueling.

There were news reports after the raid that the attack planes flew in a tight formation across Saudi Arabia to look like an airliner on radar and the pilots deceived Jordanian and Saudi air traffic controllers by speaking in Arabic.

The stories made great press and intrigue, but there was no truth to them. English is the universal language for air traffic control—not the native tongues of whatever country the flight happens to be over.

The strike settled a worldwide argument. Single-engine aircraft could carry out long-range strike attacks as safely as twin-engine jets like the F-4.

18

Fallout

ALL NEWS REPORTERS have sources. Some are scattered all
over the world. When the U.S. Ambassador to Israel,
Samuel Lewis, was told of the raid, he immediately
informed the State Department in Washington.

Someone in the State Department then informed a
news friend at a Pittsburgh, Pennsylvania television
station. The station called its CBS network news headquarters in New York. And CBS New York then called its
Tel Aviv bureau and asked for verification that the IAF
had bombed the Iraqi nuclear reactor and that all aircraft
had returned safely to base.

It was 0705 Monday morning in Tel Aviv when CBS
attempted to verify this report with military sources in
Israel. They were given a flat denial.

The *Jerusalem Post* heard of the news report a short
time later. The reporter involved was ridiculed by the
sources he questioned as to the veracity of the American
report. Later in the afternoon those sources apologized,
insisting they had not been privy to the information.

Israel took a verbal beating internationally.

Regardless of how successful the raid was, Israel got
blistered by world opinion.

It only strengthened its resolve to protect itself rather
than depend on any other country for help. The need for
this raid had proven to them they could count on no

other country for help on critical issues they felt most important to their survival.

If there wasn't any radioactive fallout from the attack, there was every bit as much verbal fallout in the diplomatic and press corps. Begin made his contribution by bombastically defending the need for the attack and the dire consequences if it wasn't carried out.

Péres was angry in his allegations of political intrigue on the part of Begin staging the attack just before the elections to enhance the Likhud party's chances for victory.

And the rest of the world professed shocked indignation over the raid, yet deep down there were many relieved political leaders and governments.

Two hours and five minutes after the attack, Menachem Begin called U.S. Ambassador Lewis. Lewis's reaction: a laconic "You don't say." But he promptly relayed the information to Washington.

Begin had hoped Washington might release the news, which would have spun the United States into the web of involvement with Israel in the attack. Such an action would have taken some of the heat off Israel. The Reagan administration didn't take the bait.

The Israeli Cabinet had instructed, and Begin agreed, no release of information until it came from another source.

The media in all Arab countries was monitored by Israeli intelligence and the military for some scrap of information about the raid.

Begin was anxious to get the word out, especially since everything had been so successful. It's believed that at this point, whatever doubts he may have had before the raid, he now wanted to make political hay out of the success.

Then around Monday noon it happened.

There was a speech given by the Jordanian prime minister in a public debate in the Jordanian Parliament accusing Israeli planes of cooperating with Iran in the Iraq-Iranian war.

Word was flashed to Begin. He reacted impetuously.

Instantly, and without further analysis, he went public with his announcement.

Events were to later show the Jordanian debate had nothing to do with the reactor raid, but was standard routine verbiage attacking Israel. Even Iraq had been in a quandary as to who had staged the raid.

The air defense system of Iraq was so poorly operated they had no idea who the culprits were. Israel could have let Iran get the blame. That was the most likely suspect to Iraq. But like anyone impatient to do what he wanted to do, Begin had reacted to what he wanted to hear.

Was it pride? Was it for political purposes? Was it for vindication? Was it to intimidate other Arab countries about Israel's convictions and commitment that there would be no nuclear capabilities in the Middle East by her enemies?

It was probably all of the above.

The Iraqi ambassador to Italy, Taha Ahmed Ad Daud, held a news conference five days after the raid.

He freely admitted his government had no idea who was responsible for the attack until the Israeli admission.

Once Iraq found out who staged the damage to its nuclear facilities, the Revolutionary Command Council of Iraq issued a statement on Monday evening.

Using all the venom and poisonous words they could muster, Iraq flailed at Israel and the surprise raid which they branded as aggression. But there was little they could do except generate all the political ill will possible for Israel.

Saddam Hussein had lost face because of the successful and undeterred attack by his archenemy Israel. He wasn't to be seen or heard from until ten days after the attack.

In his first public reaction to the raid on June 23, the Iraqi president called on "all peace-loving nations of the world to help the Arabs in one way or another acquire atomic weapons" to balance what he called "Israel's nuclear capability."

Hussein also declared that "no power can stop Iraq from acquiring technological and scientific know-how to serve its national objectives."

This attitude would later be cited by Begin as further vindication for the raid.

Angry debate flared throughout Israel with the presidential election just three weeks away.

Other Begin comments besides revelation of the attack stirred passions and engulfed the small country in strong political arguments.

Begin held a crowded news conference in Jerusalem the Tuesday after the raid. He was flanked by IDF Chief of Staff Rafael Eitan, Air Force Commander David Ivri and Military Intelligence Chief Yehoshua Sagi.

It was a stormy, emotional, defiant and forceful presentation by Begin. His defense of the mission was vintage Begin.

"Despite all the condemnations heaped on Israel for the last 24 hours," he began, "Israel has nothing to apologize for. Ours is a just cause, we stand by it, and it will triumph. It was an act of supreme moral, legitimate national self-defense."

He said that he would stress this point if the United States questioned the alleged misuse of American weaponry in the raid.

"This Sunday's air force action against the Iraqi reactor was literally a lifesaving operation.

"I've lived with this thing for two years," Begin continued, "and I wouldn't wish it on anyone.

"Sometimes," he said, when he would meet and chat with little children, "suddenly I would be struck by the thought: 'My God, what's going to happen to those children in a few years' time . . . an atom bomb will fall on them.'"

Begin said Churchill's famous declaration after Dunkirk was appropriate to express the Israeli nation's debt to its own air force—'those wonderful young men': "Never have so many owed so much to so few."

Begin revealed that the decision to bomb the reactor

had been made "many months ago." But there had been "obstacles and problems" which repeatedly caused delays.

Chief of Staff Rafael Eitan had told him yesterday, the premier added, that the operation had been executed "with 100 percent perfection—not one percent less."

Iraq's President Saddam Hussein, a "very cruel" ruler who had butchered his closest colleagues, would have had "no hesitation in dropping three or four or five of those bombs on Israel," Begin declared.

"They would have pulverized Israel's population centers, destroyed its industrial infrastructure and decimated its army."

He reiterated that for the last two years he had lived with the "horrible thought" of Israel perishing in a nuclear holocaust launched by Iraq, but since the destruction of the reactor, "I feel like a man who's left prison. I feel like a free man."

In spite of the bitter reelection campaign, Begin said any future Israeli government would follow "the precedent we created" and destroy the Iraqi reactor if it is rebuilt.

Begin added that, according to the "specialists' estimates" of how long Iraq would need to refurbish the facility, he himself would no longer be around to give the order. But he was sure Israel would strike once again to destroy the reactor.

"Never again will there be another Holocaust," Begin said, recalling the 6 million Jews killed by the Nazis during World War II.

"If the nuclear reactor had not been destroyed," Begin stated, "another holocaust would have happened in the history of the Jewish people. There will never be another holocaust in the history of the Jewish people.

"Never again! Never again!"

Referring to the hostile comments that the operation triggered abroad, Begin said, "We do not fear any world reactions. I say this in all frankness."

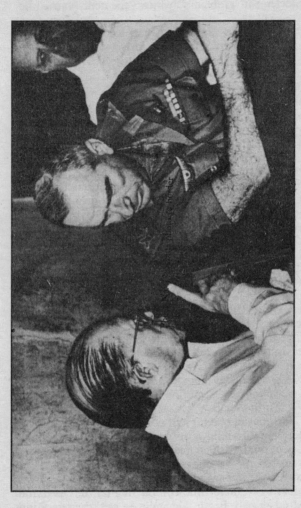

Prime Minister Menachem Begin makes a point with Army Chief of Staff Lt. General Rafael Eitan prior to briefing the Israeli Knesset (parliament), Foreign Affairs and Defense Committee two days after the raid on the Iraqi nuclear reactor.

(UPI/Bettmann Newsphotos)

He said he had sent a letter to President Reagan on Monday outlining Israel's decision and need for the raid.

"We shall stand firm in the face of any criticism from any quarter to ensure the existence of our people in its homeland," he said. Begin continued that Israel would act "with all the means at our disposal to protect our people" from the threat of nuclear weapons.

The prime minister was frank in discussing the far-reaching policy implications of this action.

Israel, he said, would not tolerate "any" enemy having a nuclear weapons capability. "I didn't say 'any Arab state,' I said 'any enemy'," Begin carefully corrected the questioner at the news conference.

His comments were left open to either or both of two interpretations: Egypt is not an "enemy" and, therefore, her nuclear program will not be disturbed. Pakistan, though not "Arab," is an "enemy" and so her nuclear program stands in danger of Israeli action. Libya, at any rate, qualifies under both interpretations—"Arab" and "enemy"—and Begin implied she is high on Israel's hit list.

Asked specifically if this policy was directed against Libya which is reportedly trying to acquire nuclear weapons, Begin, amid much laughter, gave a much-quoted reply: "Let's first deal with the meshuggener [crazy man] Saddam Hussein. The other meshuggener [Libyan strongman Moammar Gadhafi] we'll deal with another time."

The generals at the news conference were tight-lipped about the operation. But Ivri did confirm publicly that the pilots had trained for many months, the operation had gone according to plan so much so that the debriefing was "relatively boring," no new bombs had been used and certain "technical devices" had been "developed" and "affixed to the planes."

When asked to compare the Iraqi attack to what was perceived necessary to knock out the dangerous Syrian SAM missiles placed in Lebanon, he said the operations would be "like comparing a tomato to a cucumber."

Ivri concluded, "The main thing is that this attack we have already completed successfully, whereas the other one is still ahead of us."

Then he quoted the Old Testament: "One who puts on his armor should not boast like one who takes it off."

"Bravo!" exclaimed Begin.

Begin said the Israeli pilots had "no possibility of making a forced landing over enemy territory if they got in trouble," surrounded by antiaircraft guns, surface-to-air missiles and fighter planes.

"And yet they went into the lions' den to defend our Jewish people," he said.

When asked if it was true the pilots had been told they were on a possible suicide mission, Begin bristled, saying, "They did not go in there to die. They went in there to save our people. It was risky, but very, very logical."

Begin said that Israel would be prepared to sign the Nuclear Nonproliferation Treaty after the Arab states have signed a peace treaty with Israel. He also reiterated Israel's position that Israel will not be the first country to introduce atomic weapons into the Middle East.

The premier claimed that he had received many telegrams from the United States and other parts of the world congratulating Israel on the action.

He also intimated he knew there was a difference between the private opinions of some world leaders and the public statements they made rebuking the Israeli attack.

At one point, Begin was asked what would happen if the world condemned Israel.

"Well, my friends," he said, "what can we do? We are an ancient people, we are used to it. We survived, we shall survive."

When asked during a radio interview what kind of world reaction to the raid he expected, Begin said, "We will understand all the reaction, because what we did was defend ourselves. We warned the French; we told them not to continue to supply the Iraqis with this equipment."

Asked about Arab reaction, Begin replied, "I don't care about the Arab world. I care about *our* lives."

His flair for fiery, bombastic rhetoric was at its best following U.S. Secretary of Defense Caspar Weinberger's desire for stern action against Israel and the delivery delay of four F-16s. It was in a speech to a group of students at Petah Tikva School.

"What kind of morality do you operate under, Mr. Secretary of Defense?" asked Begin. "They wanted to drop nuclear bombs on us. They wanted to destroy our children, as a million and a half youngsters were slaughtered in the Holocaust.

"You, Mr. Secretary of Defense, are punishing the side which protected itself, and rewarding the murderous dictatorial aggressor. If anyone tries to manufacture instruments of mass destruction against us, we shall destroy them," Begin declared to the sound of tumultuous applause and chants.

"How can Labor accuse us of using the destruction of the nuclear reactor as an election ploy? Would I ever send Jewish pilots to a possible death—or to a fate worse than death—which captivity and torture would be?" he asked.

The audience roared back, "No!"

Begin continued, "The chief of staff, the air force commander and the military intelligence chief are not Likud members. Would they endorse and embark on such a risky venture to help us win the election?"

In a later interview with London's *Sunday Telegraph,* Begin denied ordering the raid to win the June 30 election.

"What calumnies!" he exclaimed. (Webster's defines "calumny" as the act of uttering false charges or misrepresentations maliciously calculated to damage another's reputation.)

"What people must realize is that, election or no election, the government of a country has to go on and vital issues must be faced."

To a great extent, all the angry words and rhetoric following Operation Babylon was part of a rite of protest by all countries concerned. One politician described it as, "everybody's going through the motions."

The raid so close to the election put Shimon Péres in an untenable position. He began to appear increasingly tired and disconsolate. Most of Israel was euphoric about the effort to protect their country.

Yet despite all the denials, there were strong feelings that politics played a part in the timing. Although the raid came in the midst of an election campaign, political leaders representing a broad spectrum of ideology rallied behind the government to support the raid.

Péres' response to the raid was guarded, and for the most part, supportive. What else could he do but praise the air force for the "brilliantly planned and executed" mission?

"Once again, the Israeli Air Force showed it is the best in the world," he said.

But he stopped short of endorsing the mission explicitly.

As William Claiborne reported in the *Washington Post:*

"The potential impact of the raid on the outcome of the election may explain the extraordinary flurry of public statements by Begin about the details of the bombing and the condemnations by foreign governments."

"He's making a virtue out of a necessity," one of his aides said, adding, "Find me one Israeli on the street who thinks that that reactor should still be there."

"What is his next surprise?" a seemingly dispirited Péres asked bitterly at a press conference.

Meanwhile, in the United States news of the raid flashed around the country with explosive reactions. There were questions about why U.S. intelligence didn't know about it in advance. Second, it put President Reagan in an awkward position.

He had always been sympathetic with Israel's balance

of power and survival. And throughout this whole incident it would be the president who was the most sympathetic toward Israel. His State Department was prepared to virtually desert Israel.

Yet, he had to condemn the use of American-made warplanes for such a surprise attack. To keep his credibility with the Arab world and his efforts alive to try and solve the larger problems of Middle East peace, action was necessary.

The president approved U.S. participation in a UN resolution condemning Israel, although he wanted no part of putting teeth in it such as sanctions.

Reagan reassured Israeli Ambassador Ephraim Evron in Washington that U.S.-Israeli relations would not be affected by the attack. But some punishment was called for. So delivery of four F-16s ready for delivery to Israel from the Fort Worth General Dynamics plant was stopped until it was determined whether the U.S.-built aircraft were used in violation of the U.S. Arms Exports Control Act which states such equipment must be used for defensive purposes. The issue was never specifically resolved.

This effort was aimed to chastise Israel without having a significant effect. It was more symbolic than damaging. Nevertheless, Begin attacked the action as unjust.

But the temporary freeze brought plenty of concern over Israel's longstanding life and death dependence upon the United States for weapons. Since Israel became a nation in 1948, Washington has provided more than $14 billion in military assistance. That makes Israel second only to Vietnam as recipient of American arms aid.

The quarantine stayed in effect until September 1.

The French reaction to the air strike, although angry, was fairly low-key, in spite of the fact that they had supplied the Iraqis with the reactor and had a technician killed as the only reported casualty of the raid.

Newly elected French President François Mitterrand condemned the raid: "Any violation of the law will lead to our condemnation. Whatever may be our feelings for Israel, this is the case now concerning the intervention decided by Israeli leaders against Iraq, which has led to the death of one of our compatriots."

Foreign Minister Claude Cheysson said: "I am saddened. This government has a great deal of sympathy for Israel, but we don't think such action serves the cause of peace in the area."

He also declared that the Israeli attack was "unacceptable, dangerous and a serious violation of international law."

In a television interview, he noted that nuclear cooperation with Iraq had stopped and would be subject to tight French controls if it resumed.

"We have no nuclear cooperation that could be diverted to military ends and we will double, triple and quadruple our controls," Cheysson concluded.

There also was a sense of relief in the back rooms of French power that the reactor was gone.

Cheysson had already stated, "We socialists would never have signed this contract [for the plant]. At least not without a clearer idea of Iraqi intentions. And not without clearer guarantees that it could be used only for peaceful purposes."

The raid did have a positive effect on nuclear proliferation. And there was no serious long-term detrimental effect between French and Israeli relations.

Immediately following the raid, the French pulled out 115 of their nuclear scientists in Iraq, leaving behind 15 in Baghdad to survey possible radiation problems resulting from the attack. But there were no problems.

The Italian Foreign Ministry expressed "serious concerns" over the attack. When all the bomb news hit world headlines, the Italians started back-pedaling their support of Iraq. The head of the National Commission for Nuclear Energy said he would recommend that Italy stop helping Iraq build nuclear research laboratories if the Arab nation's intentions were not peaceful.

"If it is true that the head of state of Iraq has made a statement in favor of an atomic bomb, then I will recommend to the government to interrupt the program," Umberto Colombo, the commission's president, told the Associated Press.

The usually blunt British Prime Minister, Margaret Thatcher, stated, "Armed attack in such circumstances cannot be justified; it represented a grave breach of international law."

President Anwar Sadat of Egypt felt bushwhacked. Here only three days before, he had met with Begin in a much publicized head of state conference and now, because of that meeting, it appeared Sadat was in cahoots with Israel in the raid.

He exploded, personally calling the Israeli action "unlawful" and "provocative" and warned it could only set back the search for a comprehensive peace. More than personally being concerned about the raid, he was mad about how it made him look to his Arab brothers.

Egyptian Foreign Minister Kamal Hassan Ali branded the Israeli attack as "an act of international terrorism that cannot be accepted. It is a flagrant aggression that cannot be justified."

The Egyptian Parliament voted to ask the United States to reconsider its military aid to Israel. But despite all the Egyptian noise, the raid did not seriously affect the Israel-Egyptian peace process. Sadat was locked into the Camp David agreement to get all the Sinai Peninsula back—and he did.

Syria urged international censure of the Israeli strike.

"The Arab Republic of Syria has warned more than once about the Zionist enemy aggressions and its constant aggressive nature that constitutes a dangerous threat to the Arab nations and peace in the region," a Syrian spokesman said.

King Khaled of Saudi Arabia reportedly telephoned Iraqi President Saddam Hussein to express his disapproval of the bombing. But the Saudis' public reaction was muted. Apparently they were relieved that Iraq was no longer within relatively easy reach of building a nuclear bomb.

The incident lent credence to the arguments of the Saudis, whose airspace was so easily violated by the Israelis, that they needed AWACS surveillance planes from the United States to protect themselves.

King Hussein of Jordan also phoned the Iraqi president to condemn the Israeli action and express Jordan's support.

The PLO announced its support of Iraq and said Israel's aim was military control of the Middle East.

Kuwaiti State Minister for Cabinet Affairs, Abdul Azi Hussein, called the Israeli move "another proof of the acts of terrorism practiced by Israel in the region."

An editorial in the Abu Dhabi newspaper, *al-Ittihad,* complained that all the Arabs seemed likely to do about the Sunday raid was fire "word bullets" at Israel.

In a similar vein, a cartoon in one Kuwaiti newspaper showed Arab guns firing diplomatic declarations at Israeli planes.

"We are incapable of acting," said one member of Kuwait's National Assembly. "We are too divided to be able to contain Israel for another decade at least."

The United Arab Emirates, Bahrain and Morocco also joined the chorus denouncing the attack.

Friends and helpers of the Entebbe rescue, Kenya, issued a government statement describing the attack as "unwarranted . . . indefensible. Whatever the justification, it had served no other purpose than further escalation of tension in the area."

The Argentine Foreign Ministry called the raid a threat "to the peace and security in the Middle East."

The Greek Foreign Minister called the attack "unacceptable."

The West German Foreign Ministry said it was "dismayed and concerned" by the attack.

Budding nuclear power Pakistan, worried about a

similar threat from nuclear enemy India, blasted the raid as "an act of international gangsterism" and said it posed a serious challenge to the Islamic world.

The Chinese Foreign Minister, Huang Hua, said the Israeli leaders were "gangsters and venomous enemies of world peace."

Japan, heavily dependent on Middle East oil, said in a statement by Foreign Minister Sunao Sonoda that "Israel's action cannot be justified under any circumstances."

Iran, at war with Iraq for nearly a year and the country that tried to destroy the reactor first, condemned the action and said in a statement it was, "a United States conspiracy carried out by its regional accomplice, the Zionist regime."

United Nations Secretary General Kurt Waldheim called it a "clear contravention of international law."

In Moscow, the Soviets did everything they could to tie in the United States with the raid. A Tass news agency said "billions of dollars flow in a continuous stream from the banks of the Potomac into the Israeli treasury to finance the Israeli aggression.

"It appears that the American zealots of international justice believe they and their Israeli protégés are above any law and any generally accepted international order."

The Soviet statement said the Israeli raid proved that the Reagan administration's campaign against international terrorism was a ploy.

"It is hardly possible to find a more vivid and fresh example: Tel Aviv openly carries out an aggressive act of terrorism on the level of state policy while Washington supplies it with arms and provides it with political cover," the Tass statement continued.

"The forces of peace should curb aggression in the Middle East, and the bandit raid of Israeli aircraft on the capital of Iraq is resolutely condemend in Soviet leading circles."

The International Atomic Energy Agency in Vienna condemned Israel for the raid and recommended that it be denied technical assistance and be considered for suspension from the agency.

The only country to call for blood was Libyan leader, Col. Moammar Gadhafi. He called on all the Arabs to blow up the Israeli reactor at Dimona in the Negev.

The raid offered the habitually feuding Arab leaders a new chance to find a common cause to unite against—and that was their common enemy—Israel.

Israeli officials summarized much of the critical reaction:

"After any successful operation, there is always a little fever, but the patient will be better for it in the end."

The first chapter on one nation's efforts to use conventional weapons for the destruction of the nuclear capability of another country has come to a close.

Chilling moral and strategic questions remain. What if other nations follow the Israeli lead? The Soviets have long eyed the Chinese nuclear installation of Lop Nor. India could be tempted to blow up the secretive Pakistani nuclear development in Kahuta. The volatile situation in South Africa could have an enemy neighbor attempt to destroy their reactor at Pelindaba.

Most doubt such actions would happen. But in spite of all the warning signs, the Israeli attack seemed to catch everyone by surprise.

The attack did serve to highlight the proliferation of nuclear weapon technology and the inadequacy of the IAEA's operations. And it bought a few years of safety from the possibility of an egomaniac, terrorist, crazy dictator who had proven that he had no respect for human life.

What effect such transfer has on the modern day world remains to be seen. There's no question some Arab states will continue to push for an Arab bomb. Not one of them wants to leave the Israeli nuclear threat unchallenged.

But likewise, since it takes only one trigger to set off the bomb, they are suspicious of their Arab brothers—all of whom have been enemies of each other at one time or another.

19

Epilogue

THERE'S NO QUESTION the Iraqis want to rebuild the reactor. Their national pride demands it. But as yet, it still sits in ruins.

Iraqi soldiers turn back anyone trying to get within sight of the facility. The rubble of the cupola dome has partially been cleared.

The damage from the raid was so severe, according to Jacques Rimbaud, a French technician employed by one of the main contractors, "that the central building is destroyed, the atomic reactor is damaged and the antiatomic shelter has vanished. If they want to resume work, they will have to flatten everything and start from scratch."

However, the welds of the swimming pool or tank of the reactor seem intact. Of course, they would have to be checked to ensure internal integrity of the reactor.

The large part of the dome and upper floor fell into the pool, but since it was filled with water, the damage done by the debris was cushioned by the water as it sank in the reactor tank. Apparently no water leaked out. The guts of the reactor would have to be replaced and the building leveled to be rebuilt.

It would take about three years to rebuild, and cost between $150 and $200 million.

And one of the chief hurdles in rebuilding would be money.

The war with Iran has economically crippled Iraq. By the end of 1985, Iraq had spent $35 billion of its foreign currency reserves and increased international foreign debt to $40 billion to buy equipment to fight the war.

The six years of war with Iran has cost Iraq an estimated 70,000 dead, 150,000 wounded and 50,000 POWs—all that with a population of 13 million people. It has sapped Hussein's economic strength and his ability to overcome the Israeli attack.

Iraq and Iran are trying through a war of attrition to bleed each other to death both physically and economically.

Saudia Arabia provides $4 billion and Kuwait $2 billion a year in subsidies to Iraq (supposedly loans to be repaid with oil at a later date). So taking on capital projects is difficult for Iraq. A $1 billion overhaul of the Baghdad sewage system was suspended in December 1982. The Korean laborers on the project were shipped home.

But probably chief among the problems in getting the project started again is France's refusal to sell parts and highly enriched uranium to Iraq that would allow production of plutonium and nuclear bombs. Hussein just does not have enough skilled manpower in his country to do it.

Because of his repressive regime, he has had a serious brain-drain problem with his technical experts and physicists.

Other Iraqi scientists want to stay in the Arab world and are sitting in countries like Kuwait—but don't want to be in Iraq.

After the destruction of Osirak, the French promised to assist Iraq in rebuilding the reactor, but with strengthened safeguards and the use of low-enriched uranium fuel for the reactor.

Iraq opposed this plan on the grounds it did not meet the conditions of the original contract and that the neutron flux resulting would have been lower and inadequate for certain types of research operations.

Despite Israeli threats to bomb the reactor again if any attempt were made to rebuilt it, Iraqi President Hussein has reaffirmed plans to do so.

Early on, Saudi Arabia offered to help finance reconstruction.

This time, the French hung tough on conditions that the project would be "internationalized" by ensuring the new administrative scientific director would be a Frenchman or a representative of the IAEA, and safeguards would be "doubled or quadrupled." The French had gotten themselves in a real bind over their greed for oil or insecurity.

Now with a glut on the world market, they could save some face politically and worldwide, and rectify their mistakes of nuclear proliferation.

Before the 1980 Iranian-Iraqi war, Iraq supplied France with more than 20 percent of its imported crude oil; but by December 1980 that percentage had fallen to 3.6 percent.

There was also some speculation that the dramatic raid may have jarred some other Western countries out of a pattern or willingness to trade technology for fuel to any dictatorship that wants to have its own bomb.

No agreement has been reached at this point. Fuel shipments from France apparently have not occurred.

Israeli officials were quick to renew their vows to stop any Arab country from acquiring nuclear weaponry.

"Israel will not be able to tolerate the existence of nuclear weapons in the hands of those who seek its destruction," Israeli Army Chief of Staff Lt. Gen. Rafael Eitan said in a speech given not long after the raid.

Expressing confidence that the raid crippled Iraq's nuclear capability for five to ten years, Eitan said, "Should the ambition to produce nuclear weapons recur, not necessarily in Iraq, Israel would not be able to tolerate it."

Had Hussein not taken on archenemy Iran, he could be busily rebuilding his bombed-out nuclear facilities to try and beat Arab rival Moammar Gadhafi's effort, through Pakistan, to threaten hated Israel with nuclear extinction.

Meanwhile, Israel has worked hard to repair its ties with the French.

Like so many international incidents, this one dominated the front pages for weeks, and then faded as new and different problems cropped up worldwide.

But the problems of nuclear weaponry are far from resolved and will continue to surface, but not likely with the surprise that followed the Israel Air Force's Operation Babylon.

On June 7, 1981, Israel did more than demonstrate it has the most combat-experienced air force in the world, capable of defending itself against all hostile neighbors. On that Sunday as the sun set, Israel did the world a favor.

Treasured drawing given to Air Force leader General David Ivri by the men who flew the mission as a memento of the highly successful raid. An autographed inscription not shown in the upper left corner stated "To the conductor of the Opera from the players."

ABOUT THE AUTHOR

Dan McKinnon is a former Navy pilot who has flown 64 different types of aircraft including the P-40 War Hawk and the latest and hottest U.S. fighters, including the F-15, F-16 and F-18 plus the high altitude U-2/TR-1 spy plane.

He holds the U.S. Navy helicopter peacetime rescue record of 62 air-sea saves.

For 23 years he owned and operated two radio stations in San Diego and spent four years as a newspaper publisher in La Jolla. He is also the minority owner of three television stations. He has served as president of the Country Music Association in Nashville.

A strong believer in marketplace economics, McKinnon was appointed by President Ronald Reagan in 1981 as Chairman of the Civil Aeronautics Board (CAB). He ran the agency and oversaw implementation of airline deregulation during the tumultuous period of bankruptcies and adjustment from a government-regulated industry to one controlled by the marketplace. He also played a key role in U.S. international aviation policy and negotiations for air route agreements with countries around the world.

To complete airline deregulation, at the end of 1984 McKinnon oversaw the shutdown of the CAB—the only government regulatory agency ever closed.

McKinnon has traveled extensively throughout the world and has specialized in Middle East affairs for the past 15 years.

BIBLIOGRAPHY

Jack Anderson. Various stories and columns. Washington, D.C., 1978–82

Captain M. Thomas Davis, U.S. Army. "The Politics of Begin's Baghdad Raid." *Naval War College Review:* Naval War College, Newport, R.I., March–April 1982

Lou Drendel and Capt. Don Carson. *F-15 Eagle in Action.* Carrollton, Texas: Squadron/Signal Publications, 1976

David Eshel. *Israeli Air Force 1984.* Hod Hasharon, Israel: Eshel-Dramit Ltd., 1984

Bert Kinzey. *F-16 Fighting Falcon in Detail and Scale.* Fallbrook, Calif., Aero Publishers, 1984

Tim LaHaye. *The Beginning of the End.* Wheaton, Ill.: Tyndale House, 1980

Hal Lindsey. *The Late Great Planet Earth.* New York: Bantam Books/Zondervan, 1979

_____ *The 1980's: Countdown to Armageddon.* New York: Bantam Books, 1981

_____ *A Prophetical Walk Through the Holy Land.* Eugene, Oregon: Harvest House, 1983

Roger F. Pajak. "Nuclear Status and Policies of the Middle East Countries." Current News-Special Edition *International Affairs.* Washington, D.C., February 14, 1984

Amos Perlmutter, Michael Handel and Uri Bar-Joseph. *Two Minutes Over Baghdad.* Gorgi Books/Vallentine, Mitchell & Company Ltd., 1982

Trudy Rubin. Richard C. Wilson. *The Christian Science Monitor.* June 24, 1981

Robert L. Shaw. *Fighter Combat, Tactics and Maneuvering.* Annapolis, Maryland: Naval Institute Press, 1985

Colonel William D. Siure, Jr. and William G. Holder. *General*

Dynamics F-16 Fighting Falcon. Fallbrook, California: Aero Publishers, Inc., 1976

Yigael Yadin. *Masada, Herod's Fortress and the Zealots' Last Stand.* London: Weidenfeld and Nicolson, 1966

"Arab Israel Conflict." *The Middle East Journal.* Washington, D.C.: Middle East Institute, Summer/Autumn 1981

"Technology Transfer to the Middle East." Office of Technology Assessment. Congress of the United States. Washington, D.C., September 1984

The Holy Bible

Electronic Warfare. *Jane's Weapon Systems 1984–85.* London: Jane's Publishing Company, 1985

Mobile Guided SAM's. *Jane's Weapon Systems 1984–85.* London: Jane's Publishing Company, 1985

Facts on File. New York, New York: World News Digest, September 16, 1980

Modern Fighting Aircraft F-16. New York, New York: Salamander Books, Ltd., 1983

Geography. Israel Pocket Library. Jerusalem: Keter Publishing, 1973

History until 1880. Israel Pocket Library. Jerusalem: Keter Publishing, 1973

Holocaust. Israel Pocket Library. Jerusalem: Keter Publishing, 1974

Immigration and Settlement. Israel Pocket Library. Jerusalem: Keter Publishing, 1973

Department of State Bulletin. Volume 81/Number 2053, August 1981

F-16 Fighting Falcon in Action. Carrollton, Texas: Squadron/Signal Publications, 1982

Journal of Electronic Defense. Dedham, Maine: Horizon House and Association of Old Crows, November 1985

Jerusalem Post, various issues 1981, Jerusalem, Israel

Various stories. *Aviation Week and Space Technology.* 1981–82. New York, New York

Various stories. *Newsweek Magazine.* Newsweek, Inc. 1976–82

Various stories. *New York Times.* 1976–82. New York, New York

Various bylines. *The Washington Post.* 1976–82. Washington, D.C.

Various issues. *Time Magazine.* 1976–82. New York, New York: Time, Inc.

Various stories. *U.S. News and World Report.* Washington, D.C., June 1981

Various stories. *The Wall Street Journal.* New York, New York, June 1981

Various flight, weapons and tactics guides for F-4, F-16 USAF